Grimaulkin

L. A. Jacob

Cover artwork by L. A. Jacob

Cover design by Niki Lenhart
nikilen-designs.com

Published by Paper Angel Press
paperangelpress.com

ISBN 978-1-944412-76-0 (Trade Paperback)

10 9 8 7 6 5 4 3 2

FIRST EDITION

ONE

FREEDOM 2000

T HE AIR WAS CLEAN OUT HERE, making me think of renewal and rebirth. I stood outside, taking in a deep lungful, closing my eyes to better feel the microscopic bits of pure summer heat hanging in the air, ready to burst forth in a month or two.

"C'mon, man, I ain't got all day!"

I snapped open my eyes to focus on the cabbie standing next to his yellow car. He was the first man I set my eye on here outside. Glaring at me was a tall, dark man with a Yankees baseball cap.

"Just a minute," I said, and did what I said I wasn't going to do: I looked back.

The door clanged shut behind me, its iron bars sliding into the side wall. I heard echoes of more cold iron being bolted into place, to keep the men and women inside. I don't know what I thought I was going to see in looking backward. Someone waving goodbye from one of the high windows of the cells?

"Come ON."

The driver got in the car when I moved toward the cab. I suppose the cab and the $50 in my pocket was the least the prison could do for me after I'd been their guest these last five years. Now, due to my reaching the adult age of 18, I was free.

I got into the back of the car. It smelled of cigarettes and abused leather. I hadn't even shut the door before the driver took off from the front door of the William F. Blackstone Prison. I looked up at its brick facade. Maybe it was a little lighter than I remembered it. There were no bars on the outer windows, beyond which were the offices and visitors' rooms (hardly used). The guards could retreat there if a riot ever broke out. Not that one ever happened while I was there.

The circular drive let me take a good long look at the building before the cab shot out like a bullet, heading to the wrought iron gates. I glanced at the guard who waved us through. I didn't know him. What did I expect? A "Hey, good luck, Mike"?

The very second I crossed the threshold of the outer gate, I felt the magic.

It was power, pure and simple, that surrounded the prison. Inside Blackstone Prison, there were obvious — and hidden — runes and markings to stop magic from being used by the prison's occupants. That didn't stop people from talking about magic. Or practicing some theories.

To see if the magic was active out here, I spread out my hand on my lap so that the driver couldn't see, and concentrated on the center of my palm. I felt it grow hot, then a small flame appeared.

I quickly quenched the flame and looked up at the driver, who was looking at me through the rear-view mirror, as I expected.

"You're goin' to the bus station, right?"

"Right," I said.

That's what they told me when they gave me these clothes that didn't fit. I knew they were from other — possibly dead — prisoners. I wore a long-sleeved button-down blue shirt with the Polo logo in faded blue above the right breast, threadbare at the elbows. The pants were two sizes too big and, if I didn't have the belt, they would have been down around my knees. The shoes were also too big, but at least I didn't feel like I was wearing clown shoes.

There was no way I would have fit into the clothes I came in with. There's not much to do in prison other than read and work out. Since reading material wasn't exactly prolific — I read *Stranger in a Strange Land* eight times and hated it each time — I'd pushed myself to the limits and beyond in the gym.

"What were you in for?" the cabbie asked.

I looked out the window.

"You don' wanna talk about it?"

"No. I don't."

"How long were you there?"

"Five years."

"Oh, that's nothing."

"Yeah. Easy for you to say." I glared at him through the rear-view mirror. "I'm not exactly in the best mood for conversation."

"Jeez," he muttered, looking away.

As the cabbie shut up and drove, I looked out at the quiet world. I put the window down; it only went about half way before stopping. It was enough, I suppose.

I could smell the fields of upstate New York — animal smells of cow and horse dung. Even this close to the prison there were still some domestic animals, small local farms that I would later find out could be considered "organic". I could feel the magic in the air, tingling, giving me goose bumps. I could use the magic myself if I wanted to. I could probably fly to the bus station almost as quickly as this guy was driving. However, I was let loose from prison with a simple caveat: that I could no longer summon any entities. As that was what had gotten me into trouble this time, I had agreed.

"Summoning" is a broad term in magical circles, especially with the so-called Magical Cops, the Rosicrucians. What I just did in the back seat could be considered a summoning, if I had used something outside of my body to create the fire. However, I used my own will, and my own heat, to manifest a flame. If I used my own will and energy to fly, I could probably get about twenty feet down the road before falling out of the sky. I would need an entity, something outside of my body, to keep me aloft if I wanted to fly to the bus station.

Being in prison gave me plenty of time to work on my semantics so I could argue my point if necessary — if I got caught. If I used energy and power outside of myself to augment my own abilities, was that a summoning? I could argue that it wasn't. If I had wings, then yes, I could use magic to fly. But I have legs, so I can use the energy around me to run faster (that is, if my body could handle running faster, which, in its present, well-toned condition, I supposed it could).

Of course, if it was ever found out that I was using magic in daily life, the Rosicrucians would swoop down on me like a flock of pigeons on bread. So, if I used magic, I had to keep it tightly under wraps.

We drove out of the more rural area of upstate New York into the city of Troy. The cabbie sped through the streets like he had melting ice in the backseat and had to get it to the freezer because his life depended on it. I supposed I should have talked to him, but I really wasn't in the mood to bare my soul to a cabbie. I needed to bare my soul to someone else.

This part of town was full of boarded-up properties. People of different races other than my own thronged the neighborhoods. It didn't look like a pleasant area for a white boy like me. But, if I had to, I could take care of myself. I'd learned a few things in that gym: boxing, wrestling mixed and cobbled together martial arts, and magic.

As the cabbie drove, avoiding people and cars, running yellow lights, and rolling through stop signs, I slunk a little lower in the seat. I didn't want to end up back in prison because someone looked at me like I was fresh meat and I had to defend myself.

The bus station was a square building that had been top-of-the-line … in the '50's. Now, it had a few boarded-up sections of its own. Graffiti covered the side we approached. The cabbie pulled up to the curb just behind a bus that was dropping off passengers at the front door.

"Your stop," said the cabbie.

"Thanks." I put my hand on the door. I heard a hum and saw that the window was being closed, probably from his end.

"Yeah."

As soon as I shut the door, the cabbie peeled around the bus and took off.

I thrust a hand into my pocket. The two twenties and a ten were still there.

I turned to see a set of cloudy glass doors that looked like they had been there since the Cold War. I pushed through them to the interior of the bus station.

I looked around for a paper schedule. Instead, I found the schedules displayed on large TV's attached to the wall. I had two options: go home to New Haven, and see what awaited me there; or find out if my older sister Evelyn — who we all called Evie — had stayed in Providence, after graduating Brown University.

I surrendered to the Fates — and my budget. I approached the counter. The young dark-skinned girl with straight bright red hair stood behind the counter, smiled and said, "Good afternoon. How can I help you?" I thought she looked weird with the red hair; I said nothing about that.

"How much is a one-way trip to Providence?"

"Twenty-five dollars."

"And New Haven, Connecticut?"

She consulted a screen. "Thirty-two, seventy."

"I'll take the trip to Providence."

One thing about being a wizard: a lot of times fate — the Universe, the Great Creator, God, what have you — likes to intervene for reasons that come to fruition in time. This was probably one of those times, so I let it happen.

I boarded the bus, handed over my ticket to the driver, and found a seat. These seats were far more comfortable than any in prison, that was for sure.

We left Troy and headed to the Massachusetts Turnpike. I ended up dozing most of the way to Providence, since there's only so much trees, rest areas, and cars a person can handle watching.

I woke up to see the Providence skyline in the twilight. The sun set behind me, illuminating the skyline from behind some buildings. We went past the city, two exits beyond a bit of a traffic jam, and arrived at a large bus station.

I disembarked and looked around. Magic was here, too. Lots of it. I knew the history and antiquity of the buildings powered this magic. This was the town of H. P. Lovecraft, after all.

I saw a pay phone and picked up the handle. Its line was dead. There was an entire wall of pay phones, and I tried them all. Nothing.

I noticed most people seemed to be talking to little large bullet-shaped objects they held near their ears. When they finished talking, they would sometimes close these devices like a *Star Trek* communicator, or just slip them into a pocket or purse. I'd read about these things in one of the old *Time* magazines that we had in the prison library: cellular telephones. How amazing. But it didn't help me.

Again, Fate intervened.

"You need any help?" asked a girl. She was cute, about sixteen, wearing a mini-skirt, a pink shirt with a short jacket, and thigh-high platform boots. Her makeup was thick and runny, like she'd run, or had been through a short, but intense, crying jag. I looked down at her — I didn't realize that I had gotten this tall in five years.

"I need a phone," I said. "And a phone book."

She laughed. "They don't have phone books anymore." She pulled out one of those cellular phones from a humongous tote bag she carried. "Here, use mine. Call 411."

"411," I repeated, easily memorizing the short number. I took the phone and dialed. Nothing happened.

"Press the green button."

"Oh." I did, and held the phone awkwardly to my ear. A computerized voice said, "Cingular 411. City and state, please."

"Providence, Rhode Island."

"Please state the name or business you wish to call."

"Evelyn LeBonte."

"One moment, please." There were a series of beeps. "The number is … 401-548-9664. The number again …"

"Okay—"

"Dialing."

"Oh." But I had memorized the number.

The girl looked at me, amused. Okay, so I was a tourist in this world of technology, but she would be a tourist in my world of magic. I could understand her slight grin. It seemed I had a bit of catching up to do.

The phone rang three times before picking up. "Hello, you have reached Evie and Dominic."

Goose pimples formed on my arms, hearing her voice again, I wanted to reach through the phone and somehow teleport there. I could probably do it, but not without an entity. Her voice continued, "Neither of us are home right now, so if you could leave a message after the beep, we'll get back to you."

It beeped.

"Evie. Evie, It's Mike."

I paused. What was I going to say? I heard a loud click and a whine of feedback. I held the phone away from my ear.

"Mike?"

She sounded breathless, like she had bounded across the room to get to me. I could envision her doing just that.

"Yeah." I took in a shuddering breath, holding back emotion from my voice. "Yeah, it's Mike."

"How do I know it's really you?"

"Ask me something only I would know about you."

I could hear her breathing, catching her breath. She said, in an accusatory tone, "What's my favorite color?"

I thought for a moment. "It used to be fire-engine red."

"No, no, no, that's too easy."

"Phil used to say that color made you look cheap when you painted it on your nails."

"Mi — Mikey?" I heard her swallow a sob.

"Yeah."

"Oh, my God, Mikey …"

"Yeah."

I looked at the girl. She was watching me, curious. I wondered if she could hear Evie's strangled voice.

Evie asked me, "Where are you?"

"I'm at the bus terminal in Providence."

"You wait there. I'll pick you up. I'm in a green Camry."

"I don't know what a Camry looks like. Is it a car?"

"Look for the green car. God, Mikey … Don't go anywhere!"

"I won't."

She hung up. I looked at the phone trying to figure out how to hang up.

"A Camry is a car," said the girl, as she held her hand out for the phone. I gave it to her. She pressed the red button and tossed it back into the tote. "Have you been under a rock these past few years?"

"You could say that," I said. "I appreciate you letting me use the phone."

"No worries, mate." She smiled. "I can wait with you while your friend picks you up."

"She's not my friend. She's my sister." I turned around. I noticed a hot dog cart, and my stomach growled. I hoped the girl didn't hear it. "I guess I'll wait outside."

The girl followed me out the front door, where another bus deposited a new set of passengers. We stood off to the side in the late twilight.

"What's your name?" she asked me.

"Mike."

"I'm Ashleigh."

I held out my hand; she took it. I shook her hand, being careful not to squeeze too tightly. In prison a handshake was often a small contest to see who was the strongest.

"So have you been under a rock?"

"I've been abroad."

"Where?"

"Greece."

"They don't have cell phones in Greece?"

"Not where I was. No, um …"

"Reception?"

"Yeah." I noticed her backpack. "You in school?"

"Yeah. I just came from my friend's house."

"Aren't your parents going to be worried?"

She shrugged. "Foster parents. They don't care."

"Oh, I'm sorry."

"Don't be." She stood very close to me. I could feel her nipples poking my arm.

I turned to her and gave her my most winning smile. "Ashleigh, I don't swing that way."

She pouted. "Figures."

I laughed. "I appreciate the offer, though."

"Yeah, you would." She looked me up and down. "Well, you'll have a line of guys just trying to get in your pants."

I laughed, and I think I blushed. "I'm not here for that. I'm here to see my sister."

We made small talk after that. She told me who the president was, and a little about the current state of the world. I got her to talk about her friend and her life, so I could avoid talking about mine.

I saw a green car pass by very slowly.

"There's your ride," Ashleigh said.

In my excitement, I ran down the steps and jumped into the street, right in front of the car so she could see me. The woman behind the wheel — she was a woman, now — jerked the car to a stop. I put my hands on the hood of the car, as if that would stop it from rolling. I looked up the steps to see Ashleigh going back into the bus station. I guess she didn't need to say goodbye; I didn't take it personally.

Someone beeped. I walked to the passenger side of Evie's car and pulled the door open.

"Mike?" asked Evie.

Another beep, longer this time.

"Hi," I said. She still had the beautiful blue eyes that all of us LeBonte's were blessed with. Her blond hair was pulled back into a pony tail.

"Get in," she said. "Before the guy behind me rams me."

I jumped into the car and she drove away. We were silent for a while. She kept stealing glances at me. Finally, she said, "Mike, what happened?"

"I went to prison."

"Prison!"

"I'd rather tell you at home," I said, sighing.

"We thought you ran away. We thought you were upset after Phil …"

"That wasn't quite how it happened."

She bit her lip. "I live in Pawtucket," she said. "I'm … engaged."

"So that's the Dominic guy you mentioned on your answering machine."

"He wanted to come, but I thought he'd scare you." She looked at me while stopped at a light. She laughed. "I think you're going to be the one scaring him."

"He a big guy?"

"Yeah. Six-eight, two-twenty."

I had taken down men bigger than that. "Where did you meet him?"

"School. He's from Brown, too."

"Did you graduate?"

"Of course, I did! You think Dad wouldn't let me?" She looked out into the dark. "Mom was a wreck. She still is."

"Can we talk about this when we get to your house? I don't want you to be distracted."

"What else can we talk about? You've been gone for five years, Mikey. *Five years* in prison? For what?"

"How far is your home from here?"

"A few more minutes."

"Is Dominic at your house, waiting?"

"He's at the apartment, yes. We live together."

"I gathered that." Mom and dad must be angry, if they knew. They were staunch traditionalists.

We fell silent again. I tried to listen to the radio, but it was a low hum of a voice. I turned it up. It was a station called NPR, and went into news.

"You're a news junkie?"

"Dom is," she said. "He works for a newspaper. He's a stringer."

"Stringer?"

"Writes some stories, gets paid per story. He's hoping to get into the *Pawtucket Times*."

"And what do you do?"

She shrugged. "I'm a substitute teacher."

"You guys don't have a very steady income."

"Don't start talking like Dad," she snapped. "We get by."

I looked away from her. "I'm sorry, I didn't mean to."

She sighed. "Me too. It's just that — that's what Dad always says whenever we see him. Says Dom should get a *real* job … whatever that means."

"You see Dad once, maybe twice a year?"

"If that. We'll see him for the wedding."

"When's that?"

"June 20th."

I counted on my fingers. "April, May, June … two and a half months."

"Yeah. It's really coming up fast."

She drove down a few side streets and ended up in front of a large triple-decker house with peeling brown shingles on the bottom, and white vinyl siding on the second floor.

"Oh, good, I didn't lose the parking spot."

She parallel parked in front of the house. I got out, locking the door. Evie exited her side, then ducked into the back seat and pulled out her purse. Hitching it over her shoulder, she walked up to me. Then she threw her arms around me.

I chuckled, hugging her tightly. "I've missed you so much, Evie."

"They wouldn't let you write? Or call? They do that in prison."

"Not this prison."

She pulled back, but kept her hands on my arms. "You are going to tell me everything, Mikey."

"More than you want to know, Evie. More than you want to know."

CHAPTER TWO

THE EX-CON

Evie guided me to the right side of a triple-decker apartment building, where a set of three concrete steps led to a white steel door. She unlocked it, then held it open for me. I followed her up a narrow staircase to the second floor. There, she paused at a red door with an Easter bunny taped onto it. The bunny looked a little like Snoopy from the Charlie Brown cartoons with rabbit ears. His bottom feet were in motion and he held an Easter basket on one arm. The legs were moveable.

She unlocked the door and pushed it open. "Dom?" she called out. "I'm home."

A dog barked. It sounded like a big dog. He loped into the foyer and stopped short in front of me. The dog was a large black Labrador mix, with a fan for a tail. Its hackles rose, not knowing who I was, but it probably assumed I was safe being that I was with Evie and didn't seem to be attacking her. I cautiously moved into the apartment, not wanting to scare the beast.

"Is everything okay?" I heard a man ask.

We paused in a tiny foyer. It was furnished with a small table with a bowl, and hooks to put our coats, and a small autumnal Welcome mat to place dirty shoes. Evie tossed the keys into the bowl as I looked up to see a small linebacker of a man standing just beyond the foyer's end.

"Dom," Evie said. "This is my brother, Mikey."

I nodded to him. He crossed his arms. I held out my hand, reaching past Evie. "Hi," I said.

He looked up from my hand to Evie, and then shook my outstretched hand. Like prison, it was a testing of the mettle, and I must have passed, because he pulled his hand away first.

"You better not be some con artist."

"I swear I'm not."

"It's Mikey," Evie said, looking directly at me. "You're a little bigger, but you're still my Mikey."

I smiled, blushed, and then rubbed the back of my head. "I hate to intrude on you, but I've been traveling since this morning. Do you have anything to eat?"

"I think we have a can of tuna," said Dom.

I pulled out my money. "This is all I have."

"No," Evie said, shaking her head.

"Yes." I pressed it into her hand.

She glanced at Dom, sighed, and headed to the kitchen, which was a right-hand turn off the foyer.

As I approached it, I noticed it was an open kitchen, with a counter space instead of a table, and four chairs at the counter, two on each side of it. The kitchen was about the size of my cell.

The apartment's main living area was straight ahead from the foyer, to the left of the kitchen. It was about the size of two cells. Most of its space was taken up by a sectional, a coffee table, and a TV entertainment center. There were a few inches of space between the coffee table and the TV, and very few inches between the coffee table and the couch. Next to a door which led to another room was a desk with a computer on it.

Parallel to the kitchen was the bathroom. About the size of a closet, it held a stand-up shower that probably barely fit Dom's left leg. On the left side of the living area was an open doorway, which probably led to the bedroom.

I turned my attention to Evie, who was opening the can of tuna. The dog sat, salivating at the sound of the can opener. "No, Rufus," she told the dog. "This isn't for you."

Dom kept glaring down his nose at me. "So where have you been?"

"In prison," I said.

His eyes widened. "In prison?"

"Yeah."

"For what?"

"Murder."

Dom looked like he was ready to jump me, but, like the dog, waited for Evie's reaction. Evie merely turned to stare at me. "Murder? Who?"

I looked up on the wall. Hanging there was a picture of us as a family, taken at a photographer's studio when I was 10. My mother and father were seated in the middle. My mother, her hair done up for the occasion, looked like she was trying to go for an afro but didn't have the thick, curly hair for it. Instead it presented itself as a series of tight curls pulled up on the top of her head, held by liberal amounts of hair spray. She didn't look normally like that.

My father, a Nordic brute of a man, easily dwarfed my mother. To my parents' right stood Phil, our older brother. He was six years older than me, two years older than Evie. Phil looked just like my father: blond haired, blue eyed Aryan, broad shouldered and handsome, chiseled features. He was the quintessential older brother — the jerk. He treated me like crap — Evie sometimes worse. Phillip was his father's son, not like me who was my mother's son. Phil was on the football team, worked instead of going to college, had girlfriends, drove a car … I wasn't interested in any of that. I wanted to learn magic.

And, most of all, I hated him.

"Who?" I repeated. "You'd better make that tuna sandwich, because after I tell you, you won't want me to stay here."

"Look," said Dom, advancing on me. "We don't have time for games."

I looked at him steadily. Evie had picked a good one this time. I thought he was cute: black wavy hair and black Mediterranean eyes, dark olive skin and deep, Providence/Italian voice. Yeah, I'd do him.

I looked up at the picture, then back down to Evie. "Eight people."

She stood frozen, holding the open tuna can in one hand, the dog still sitting and waiting patiently. "Oh, Mikey, how?"

"Magic."

She gave me one of those forced laughs that you do when faced with something incredulous. "Oh, come on, Mikey. I knew you were involved in that stuff, but —"

"It was a demon."

She stared. Out of the corner of my eye, I saw Dom make the sign of the cross.

I looked between the two of them, then walked slowly to her and took the tuna can from her. "You'd better sit down."

Now the dog tracked me as I opened cupboards to look for a bowl. When I found one, I turned to see Evie and Dom standing very close to each other, Dom with his arm around

Evie's shoulders. After emptying the tuna into the bowl, I moved toward the refrigerator, talking as I went.

"It all started with Mousey," I said. "You remember Mousey, right?"

"Your bully," Evie said quietly.

I nodded. The fridge was pretty bare, but there was a loaf of bread and a jar of mayonnaise in the back. "And Aunt Jane?"

Evie nodded. Dom kept holding her close, protecting her. That's what I would do, if faced with me.

"The Rosicrucians killed her." That was the only news I got about my family, and I heard it from the man that arrested me.

Dom asked, "The *who* did what?"

"Never mind," I said to them. "I'll get to that," I set the items on the counter and started making the sandwich. "So Mousey was beating me up all the time, and I'd about had it. I asked Aunt Jane, and she helped me summon a demon, just a minor one, to punish Mousey." I put a lot of mayo on the bread and in the tuna. I missed mayo. "The demon punished Mousey all right; he showed up two years later in a wheelchair. I knew I had done that."

"Coincidence," said Dom, though his body language told me that he didn't trust me.

I shrugged. I didn't bother cutting the bread, but split it by pulling it apart with my hands, like I did in prison, where we didn't have access to sharp objects — for obvious reasons. "Then it wasn't until I was thirteen that I summoned another demon. This demon was Belial. Major Duke of Hell. Third to Lucifer himself."

Evie said, "What for?"

"I was in the gym locker room. I kissed a boy. He tattled. By the end of the day, the school knew. I got the worst beating of my life that day."

I ate the sandwich to let it sink in. Man, it was good.

"So that afternoon, I went in the garage and summoned Belial."

Evie said, "They said you ran away to join a cult."

"Who said?"

"The FBI."

"Men in black? Sunglasses, the whole thing?"

Evie nodded.

"Rosicrucians, not FBI. They wanted you to think that, when they —" I used air quotes "— 'arrested' me. They actually kidnapped me and sent me to their prison." I ate the sandwich, savoring it for a minute. I swallowed. "Can I get a drink?"

"Who were the eight people?" Dom asked.

"People who beat me up."

Evie stepped out from under Dom's protection. "Oh, Mikey." She came around the counter and hugged me. Before I closed my eyes and put my arm around her, I glanced at Dom. His eyes were narrow, his arms across his chest.

I released Evie, looking up at Dom. "I know you don't trust me. I can believe it." I looked at Evie. "I swear on all that's holy that I learned my lesson. I'm not going to summon demons again."

Dom said, "Why didn't these, what did you call them? Rozi-whats — ?"

"Rosicrucians."

"Them. Why didn't they at least call your parents? Why did they have to lie?"

I said, as if explaining to a new prisoner, "It's a prison for wizards and witches. They don't want you mundanes to know that magic works." Both Dom and Evie were wide-eyed, hanging on my every word. "Can you imagine half the population of the United States messing around with magic? There would be a lot more bad apples in that bunch than the few hundred or so prisoners in the place I got shunted off to." I finished the sandwich. "I'll leave as soon —"

"No," said Evie. "No. Don't leave. I still love you."

Dom's face held no emotion. But I was sure he was reeling inside. I didn't want to cause a breakup, so I said, "No, Evie, I think I'd better —"

"You said you're not going to do that again."

"I can't," I said slowly. "I'd disappear — this time permanently."

"As in, back to jail?"

"As in, 'Shoot first, ask questions later.' They believe in the death penalty." I looked steadily at Evie. "But listen. I'll never hurt you. Or the ones you love." I looked up at Dom. "Unless someone abuses you."

Evie put a hand on my arm. "Dom's been great to me."

I put my hand on top of hers. "I figured that, or you wouldn't have decided to marry him." I smiled at Dom. "I can't use magic much, not when it's blatantly obvious and goes against the laws of physics."

"No flying or walking on water?"

"Or turning water into wine. Though I can."

"You must be a hit at parties."

I laughed. It broke the tension, finally.

Evie hugged me again. "Stay here," she said.

"I'll sleep on the couch," I said. "But would you mind if I took a shower?" It would be the first time in five years that I took a shower alone.

"No, of course not. Those the only clothes you have?"

I nodded.

Dom looked me over. He was shorter than me, a little wider. "I might have a shirt. What size shoe you wear?"

"No idea, but these are too big."

"I'll see what I got."

Evie smiled at Dom. Dom just grunted and went into the bedroom.

"I think he likes you," said Evie, gathering up the paper towel I'd put the tuna sandwich on.

"I hope so." I watched her bustle around the kitchen. "I'm not going to impose for long. Just until I get a job and other things."

"Stay as long as you like."

I motioned to the apartment. "This place is far too small." I gave Evie a quick kiss on the cheek and went to the bathroom.

When I got out of the luxurious hot shower, during which I used all their hot water, a pair of well-worn sneakers awaited me on the floor in front of the toilet. On top of the toilet lid were a folded pair of pants and a t-shirt. The t-shirt fit tightly; the pants were sweats, and just barely too short. I came out of the bathroom to see Evie making the couch into a bed.

"Hm, yeah," she said, looking me over. "The pants are too short. We'll go buy you something tomorrow."

"Sneakers fit," I said, wiggling my toes in them.

"T-shirt fits?"

"A little tight for my taste."

She smiled. "We'll go up one size."

I went over to the makeshift bed. "I swear, I won't stay long."

"Mikey, you're my brother. My long-lost, prodigal brother. I don't want you to leave."

I sat on the couch. "Let's not tell mom and dad yet. They can find out later."

"Okay," she said. She bent down and gave me a kiss on the forehead, like she used to do.

I lay on the couch. It wasn't that lumpy. Compared to the hard cot and mattress at the prison. It was like lying on a pillow. "Good night." I pulled the covers up.

"Good night, Mikey," she said, and shut off the light.

I expected to drift off to sleep immediately. Instead, I felt something staring at me. I knew who it was without opening my eyes.

"Grimalkin," I whispered. "Let me sleep."

"I will. Your sister has nice place." When he spoke, he left out *a, an* and *the*, as if they weren't necessary in his language. I snapped open my eyes.

Standing at the entertainment center was a large obsidian man with curling black horns and long black hair. He was built like me, but all chest and shoulders. His nether regions were covered in thick fur, and he seemed to have no male or female parts that I ever saw. His legs, covered in hair, tapered down to a pair of cloven hooves. He looked like an old-fashioned version of a demon. The only thing he didn't have was a tail.

He was a demon that had been able to follow me into the prison. He taught me more magic, helped me practice, reminded me to be on my best behavior, because when "we" were set free, we would be able to fulfill our destiny — whatever the Hell that meant.

In fact, he was the one who taught me the fire spell I had used in the cab. He taught me a lot of spells. The water into wine, transmutation, was easy once he explained it. In the prison, I had taken his name, but had altered it so that he wouldn't be summoned by mistake: Grimaulkin.

I glared at him. "You leave my sister alone."

He held up his hands. "Not here for your sister. Here for you."

"What do you want tonight? Can't I sleep?"

"Sleep to come. What are your plans?"

"I need to get some clothes."

"Ah. Cannot summon clothes. Must buy them?"

"Yes."

"Money. Gold." His eyes, slitted gray against white, twinkled. Oh, he knew many money spells.

"No." I sat up. "Credit cards."

Grimalkin came around the table to stand before me. "Spell of plenty. You know."

If I could get a credit card, I could put on it a Rune of Plenty that Grimalkin had taught me. The card would have unlimited funds. It was stealing, sure. But it wasn't summoning. However …

"It's magic," I said.

"Magic against reality is what draws Knights to you," he said. "You manipulate reality, but do not break it."

"Mike?" I heard Evie call from the bedroom. "You okay?"

"Sorry," I called back. "Talking myself to sleep." I knew from experience that I was the only one who could see Grimalkin usually, though some of the more sensitive wizards and witches told me they could sense a presence. I lay back down. "Let me sleep, okay? I'll let Fate help me figure it out in the morning."

"As you wish, my master," he said, and disappeared into a cloud of purple, twinkling lights.

Dom was up first. He tried to be quiet when approaching the computer desk, but I sat up, rubbing my eyes.

"Hey, sorry," said Dom.

"No, it's all right."

"I have to check my email to see if they sent me any stories."

"Sure, no problem." I hit the bathroom and when I came out, Dom was typing away on the computer. He was frowning.

"Nothing?"

"Gotta go uptown to interview some 90-year-old Jewish woman about the Holocaust. They want it on file." The printer whirred and spat out the email.

"Evie doesn't have work today?"

"Nobody called her."

In a way, that was good. I could spend all day with her.

"Hey, do you have a credit card?"

"Yeah, why?" He seemed wary.

Maybe I shouldn't use their card. I didn't know how the spell would backfire if I botched it.

"Just curious about how to get one."

"They might not give you one because you're a felon."

"Juvenile. Records are sealed."

"You still have to explain where you were for five years."

I frowned. "Yeah, I suppose there is that."

He got up. "Gonna take a shower."

I moved out of his way and headed into the kitchen. The least I could do was make them some breakfast. I found a half dozen eggs and that loaf of bread. I could have used the Cornucopia spell I knew. It would make the fridge a center of food, from anywhere and everywhere in the world, but that was a summoning of sorts.

Dom walked by, shirtless and in boxers, heading to the shower. I stuck my head in the fridge to look for more items, but there really wasn't anything. So I made an egg sandwich each for Dom and me.

Dom, now fully dressed, came over to the counter. I had already eaten my egg sandwich. He put salt, pepper, and basil on his. "Thanks for making this."

"No problem. I used to cook at home all the time."

He started the coffee maker. "You're not gonna tell your parents? Like Evie said, your mom was a wreck."

"Mom always swung to extremes." I wondered, fleetingly, how she was at my brother's funeral. Did she wail and throw herself on the coffin? How did she feel about me? Did she ever look for me? Or did she go by what the Rosicrucians said?

I clenched my fists as I thought of the Rosicrucians — my jailers. I was glad when Evie stepped out of the bedroom, her hair tousled and eyes puffy from sleep.

"Hey," she said, smiling at me. She kissed Dom on the cheek.

"I have to use the car," he said.

"Okay," she said. "We'll go shopping after you get back."

"Why don't you take the bus and call me when you get out? I'll pick you up."

She glanced at me. "Let me go to the bathroom and think about it." She hugged Dom and went into the bathroom. Dom held the smile on his face for a few more minutes before the coffee maker beeped.

He filled up a traveling mug with black coffee, sugar, and fake cream from the fridge. When Evie came out, she said, "We'll take the bus."

Dom smiled. "Okay, I'm heading out. I'll call you when I'm heading home."

"Okay, babe." They kissed in the foyer. I turned my back to them so they could have some privacy.

Two eggs were left in the carton, so I took one out. Evie was shaking her head, "No, Mike. I don't eat breakfast."

"You just drink coffee?"

She yawned. "Breakfast of champions," she said, getting a mug. "Want some?"

I had stopped drinking coffee in prison because it tasted like wet bark to me, and we didn't have condiments. "No," I said, watching her fill a cup.

She put in an ice cube to cool it and some fake creamer. "I'll check the credit card." She headed to the computer.

"Evie, um …"

"Hm?"

I suppose I would have to do it on her card. "Let me see your card."

"Why?"

"I want to try something."

She got her purse and wallet, and handed me a MasterCard. The front of the card had a kitten. The back had her signature and the magnetic stripe. "Got a permanent marker?"

"I think so," she said. She opened a drawer in the computer desk and rummaged around in it. "Here," she handed me a black Flair marker.

I held the card in my left hand, and concentrated, visualizing an unlimited credit limit, that would show up nowhere in the system, that the dollars and cents that would be charged on this card would disappear into the cyber world, never to be found.

I drew the Rune of Plenty on the back of the card, making sure the marker did not leave the card. I signed it, charging it with my will, and pushed the spell out into the rune. I opened my eyes. I could see the card glowing, pulsing green, ready for use. I waved the card to dry it and dissipate the glow.

"What did you do?"

"Gave you a higher credit limit." I handed it back to her, holding it by the edges. "Try not to touch that mark."

She took it back, putting it in her wallet. The glow disappeared. Maybe no other wizards could see it. It wasn't a summoning spell, because I wasn't calling for money. So I was within my requirements.

I grinned at her. "Let's go shopping."

We took the bus south to the Walmart in Providence. The bus was crowded, so we stood most of the way.

I was busy watching the houses go by, thinking about what I was going to do. I needed to find a job. I needed to find a place to live. I couldn't live on their good graces forever. I'm not sure if I wanted to stay in Providence or to move somewhere far away from my parents.

Evie had been choosing her colleges when I was "arrested". Brown University was her first choice, but she had applied to every college in Rhode Island, wanting to get away from my parents. She went to a college far enough away from my father but still close enough to come home at a moment's notice from my mother. Evie was four years older than me. Phil was two years older than her. I was a mistake, as my Aunt Jane put it to me one afternoon over tea, which was one reason why my father treated me the way he did.

One time, the school bus couldn't drop me off because there was no one was at the corner to get me. I still remember it like I was yesterday. I was seven. It was winter. Other kids got off the bus and I didn't. I started to cry. I wet my pants. I cried even more. The bus monitor took pity on me and said she would bring me home after the bus returned to the bus yard.

When the bus pulled into the yard, my father was there waiting. He was livid. Not because he was worried about me, but because I wet my pants in public. He spanked me and sent me to my room without supper. Then Phil added insult to injury by coming into my room and calling me a pansy, a momma's boy, a baby.

Phil could do no wrong. I was always in trouble at home. Something broke, it was my fault. I was clumsy. I preferred to stay locked up in my room with my books and music, rather than go out and play with the neighborhood kids. I cooked every Sunday with my mother — big, lavish dinners that my father would eat in the TV room during football season, and reluctantly eat with us all the other times of the year.

Evie touched my hand. I looked down at her and smiled. "What're you thinking about?" she asked.

"Nothing special," I said.

Evie and Aunt Jane didn't get along much. Aunt Jane was, to me, the only honest person in the family. My mother's sister, she lived in a high-rise in Hartford. A heavy-set woman with diabetes and gout, Aunt Jane chain-smoked and drank whiskey straight up. She was also a self-styled witch who kept trying to get the lottery numbers and hit it big someday. She had power, but Fate would deny her winning a ton of money. Fate would often give her money necessary to keep her head afloat, but otherwise never enough to buy the BMW she so craved.

The Rosicrucians told me they had to kill her, as she should have known better than to teach me how to summon demons. But she's not the one who taught me — I taught myself. The Rosicrucians didn't believe that a 13-year-old could learn such complicated magic on his own, so they had to put the blame on someone older. I wondered if her trial had been as short as mine — or if she even had one.

When we got to Walmart, half the bus disembarked. We went inside, and Evie grabbed a carriage — what everyone else in the world calls a shopping cart.

"Okay, size 2X in the shirts, right?" she asked glancing back at me, as she led the way down the aisle.

I was almost overwhelmed by the time we got to the men's department. So much stuff! We had passed through the women's department, and I was surprised at the types of clothes. The colors! The textures. I wanted to touch everything. I lagged behind Evie as I touched the smooth glitter of a woman's t-shirt, smelled the newness of a leather clutch. I heard a bird chirping somewhere above me. I looked around for the bird — was it the Rosicrucians watching me? Did they know I cast a spell on the card already?

Evie came back up the aisle and hooked her arm around mine. "Got lost?"

"Yeah. I never thought this place would be so big."

"Let's get you shoes first," Evie said. "They're right here."

We turned a corner and I saw row upon row of women's shoes. Sandals for the upcoming summer, sneakers, low boots … We walked past those to the men's shoes, which were much more boring. Loafers, sneakers, and work boots. Some ugly sandals were mixed in among them as well.

We picked out some plain high-top sneakers. It took three tries to get the size I needed. Across from the shoes was the men's clothing department. I talked her into three pairs of jeans — she only wanted to buy two — four shirts, and underwear. She bit her lip as I kept putting stuff into the carriage.

After tossing in a package of socks, I said, "I'll pay you back, if you get charged for this."

She blinked. "What do you mean, 'if I get charged for this'?"

I smiled at her."Trust me." I looked across the aisle. "Why don't you buy something for yourself?"

"No, I can't."

"I saw some nice lingerie."

She giggled and blushed. "Mike."

"For the wedding." I was such a tempter. "C'mon, it's not like you're going to be wearing it for long."

"I don't like lingerie. It's scratchy."

"Then something nice to sleep in, not one of your fiancé's old clothes."

She again bit her lip for a moment before saying, "You know what I need? A new black dress."

"Let's see if they have any."

They did, consisting of a clingy black tank and a black jacket with huge blue flowers on it. Of course, she now needed shoes, and she found a pair of sandals to go along with it.

"Now something for Dom."

"Mike, stop," Evie said. "I don't have the money for this."

I picked up a nice pair of cargo shorts. "What about these?"

"Mike, I can't —"

I tossed it in the carriage. "Let's go look at the books."

"Mike —"

"Or a library? I'll go to the library if that'll make you feel better."

She said, "Mike, there's already too much in here."

"Well, we do have to get lunch."

Evie sighed. Her phone rang a jaunty little tune. She rummaged in her purse and picked it out. "Hello? Hi, hon. Yeah, we're at Walmart. Sure, pick us up here."

"And we're going grocery shopping afterward," I said, loud enough for him to hopefully hear.

She rolled her eyes. "See you then, hon. Love ya." She hung up. "Mike, this will put me over the limit."

"Will you please trust me? Magic doesn't work if you don't believe."

"Mike." She looked ready to launch into a tirade of how magic didn't work.

I knew it worked. I had spent over ten years of my life working with magic — and the last five years in the company of wizards only proved it. What did she want? A firestorm in the middle of the stationery section?

I said, "Let me give the guy the credit card to activate the spell."

"You don't look like an Evelyn LeBonte."

"Humor me."

"No, I'll do it."

"Do you believe?"

Evie sighed. "Yes, I believe."

"You sound so convincing." I smiled and put my arm around her shoulders as we walked over to the checkout line.

I took everything out of the carriage and put them on the belt. She was biting her lip and watching the items go by. I pulled the carriage down the aisle and smiled at the checkout lady, who smiled back.

"Hi," I said. "What's a guy got to do to get a job here?"

The lady thumbed at the customer service desk. "Go over there, fill out an application."

"Do you like working here?"

She shrugged, scanning the items through and then bagging them. "It's good for extra money. I'm retired."

"Oh? You look awful young to be retired."

She blushed and smiled happily. "Early retirement. It was either that or be let go."

"From where?"

"Blue Cross."

"What did you do there?"

I kept on talking to her, as she took Evie's card and swiped it through. It was the moment of truth. I asked her about her grandkids, and the receipt popped up. It had worked!

Evie, looking a little confused, took the card and the receipt from her, and stared at the bottom number on the receipt as I gathered the bags.

"They must have increased our limit," Evie said, as we headed out the door.

"I told you."

"Mike," she said firmly. "It's not magic."

"Oh, but it's a happy coincidence?"

"I'll have to check online when we get home."

"You are going to stop at the grocery store, aren't you?"

"We're out of eggs and cereal."

"C'mon, Evie," I said. "Go real shopping for once. Wouldn't you like a thick, juicy steak, with steaming fresh mashed potatoes and corn and gravy?"

She was salivating. I know she was. I sure was. "We can't afford that."

"Yes, you can. With that thin little card."

"Mike, we have to pay it sometime."

"When I get a job, I'll give you the money."

Evie asked, "What about you?"

"What about me?"

"Don't you want to spend some money?"

"I'll put aside a little for going out, maybe books. Unless the library's within walking distance ..."

Their car pulled up to where we were waiting. Dom peered over the seat. "Hey, wanna lift?"

I shoehorned myself into the back seat along with the bags.

Dom glanced at the bags. "Just a few things?"

"A hundred and twenty dollars," said Evie with a sigh.

"We had that much on the card?"

"Evidently, we do," she said, glancing back at me. I grinned. "I think they upped our credit limit."

"How?" Dom asked. "We've been making minimum payments for months now."

"I don't know," Evie replied. "We have to stop at Shaw's and pick up some cereal and eggs."

"... and steak and potatoes and gravy and corn," I said.

Dom said, "Mmmmm."

"Don't listen to him," said Evie told him.

"C'mon, Evie. We haven't had a dinner like that in weeks. And he's our guest."

She sat back in her seat. "I'm trying to stay on what limited budget we have."

"Just once," I said. "And then tomorrow you'll have work, will that make you feel better?"

"All right, all right," she almost shouted, throwing her hands in the air in a gesture of defeat. "But don't say I didn't warn you."

CHAPTER THREE

BOOKS

I HAD NEVER SEEN EVIE LOOK SO SATISFIED AND HAPPY as when she put her fork down on the plate and let out a sigh.

"See?" Dom smiled, still sawing into his prime rib. "Wasn't this worth it?"

"I'm so full," Evie said. "But I have to check our credit limit and see what the minimum payments are going to be like now."

Dom looked at me. With his knife, he pointed at Evie. "Buzzkill."

"Responsible," she replied, poking Dom in the ribs.

I sat back, satisfied as a cat who'd had tuna and a cream chaser. Evie pushed herself from the counter and went over to the computer, firing it up.

"Bet this is the best meal you've had in a while," said Dom.

"Hell, yeah," I said. "Tomorrow, can we have chicken pot pie?"

He laughed. "You make it."

"Dom!" yelled Evie. She sounded slightly panicked.

He jumped a little in his chair and called back, "What is it?"

"Come here."

Dom left the counter. I got up to follow him, but Rufus remained at the counter, staring at it. I stayed near the table instead, just in case Rufus got it into his doggie brain to jump up and help himself to the rest of the prime rib.

"How the Hell did that happen?" Dom asked, leaning over Evie's shoulder.

"What?" I asked.

"We got a credit limit of $100,000."

I leaned back against the counter. "Told you."

Evie said, "There must be some mistake. I'll call the credit card people tomorrow —"

"Dammit, Evie!" I said. They both turned to me. "I'm trying to help here."

"You did that?" asked Dom.

"Yes, I did." I ignored the dog and the counter, and went over to the computer. "Look at the transactions. Were there any today?"

She scrolled down. "Sometimes it takes a couple of days to come through —"

"Evie, you know that's bull," said Dom. "They take our money out the same day, but when it comes to returns, it could be a week or more." Dom looked up at me. "Where did they go?"

I shrugged. "Beats me, but they're not your responsibility."

"That's stealing, Mike," Evie said.

"I consider it redistribution of wealth."

Evie turned her full body to face me. Her face was a mixture of worry and anger. "Mike. Mike, make it stop. We bought what you're wearing, and what you ate."

"She's right about stealing, Mike," said Dom. He looked at the screen. "But keep the credit limit where it is."

"Dom!"

"Emergencies."

"It's always an emergency."

I said, "Isn't it okay to have the credit companies up the limit to whatever they want? You're a good customer. You'll pay your minimum payment."

"Not if it's a thousand dollars a month," Evie said.

"It won't get that high," I said. They both now had looks of worry. I sighed and held out my hand. "Give me the card," I told her. "I'll fix it."

She got the card from her purse and handed it to me. I scratched off the Rune of Plenty as best I could. The credit limit had changed. That was permanent; it was no longer necessary for the rune to be on the card. Unfortunately, now, the charges would be put on the card. Once I scratched off the rune, the card's green glow disappeared. I handed the card back to her.

"Thank you," she said. "I don't want to see you go back into magic prison the second day you're out."

I smiled and I looked back at the table. Rufus was still staring at the chunk of prime rib. I felt bad for him, so I snuck him a hunk of meat from Dom's plate.

The next morning, the phone's ring near my head made me almost leap right off the couch. It was stupid loud. I reached over and picked it up. "Hello?"

"Hello," a woman's voice said. "Is Evelyn LeBonte there?"

I looked at the clock. It was five in the morning. This person sounded just as wide awake as I was.

Dom came out of the bedroom, looking disheveled and sexy.

"Someone wants Evie," I said.

"The school department," he called into the bedroom.

"Uh huh," Evie said. She came to the doorway and took the phone from me. "Hello? Yes. Yes. I'll be there. Thank you." She hung up. "Agnes," she said.

"I'll drop you off," Dom said. "In case."

I asked, "Agnes?"

"Agnes Little. It's the name of the elementary school." Then she yawned. "I'd better get going."

They left at 6:30, while I took Rufus out for a morning walk. Dom was seated at the computer when I returned.

"What're you going to do with yourself today?" he asked me.

"I was going to go to the library."

"About 20 minutes away in downtown," he pointed to the east, right into the rising sun's light. "You can't miss it."

An hour after that, Dom was gone, heading to his next big story. He left me a key to the house on a key ring with a bottle opener attached to it. I settled down to watch TV, figuring the library opened at ten. Rufus joined me on the couch.

"I'll take you out for a walk later, too. Okay?"

He gave me a doggie grin. I patted him. I'd never had a dog; my mother and father thought they were too much trouble. There were a lot of things my parents did ... and didn't do. They never took the bullying seriously, which made me summon those demons. My father told me to fight back. I was a skinny little thing at thirteen; I wasn't built like Phil. I couldn't fight back. I didn't know how to throw a punch. Hell, I couldn't throw a ball right, either.

Phil sometimes saved my bacon, but he never let me live that kind of stuff down. It was another reason why I hated him, though I had a myriad of reasons.

While in prison, I thought about whether what I had done was justified. In my mind, it certainly was. He treated me like crap. He was always the one the family was most proud of, winning awards for his prowess on the field. I came home with straight A's, and all I got was a pat on the head from my mother and a grunt from my father. The minute I slipped, only once in freshman science, I was seen as worthless and "not going to amount to anything".

My mother ran interference. My father would look at me and say things like, "When are you going to get taller? When are you going to try out for softball?"

My mother and I shared time together, when she showed me cooking: how to make the family recipe for apple cobbler, mashed potatoes (cream the butter first is the secret), and her special augmented mac and cheese out of a box (use half-and-half instead of milk). She also showed me how to sew, tried to show me how to knit, and taught me the basic domesticated things that girls should know.

She didn't treat me like a girl, though. She taught me how to take care of myself. I was doing laundry at seven, making dinner by ten. I also ended up cleaning up afterward and doing all the housework, in addition to my homework and projects and other school things. I never joined any extracurricular activities.

My parents worked full-time jobs. Dad was a supervisor in an insurance company. Mom worked a series of office jobs. When I was arrested, she was working for a CNA dispatch company. Phil worked in a lumberyard during summers since he turned 15, and said he'd work there right after he graduated instead of going to college.

I petted the dog and looked at the clock. It was quarter of ten, so I picked up the key, locked the door, and went down the winding stairs to the ground floor. A woman was beating a rug on a clothesline in the backyard. She turned to look at me, frowning. I waved to her. She still frowned at me. I shrugged and headed down to the sidewalk.

After walking a few blocks, I found myself out of the residential section of town and in a small area that could be considered downtown Pawtucket. I could tell it was downtown from the banks and stores along the street. There were old-fashioned glass-fronted buildings with offices above them. There was a restaurant, a coffee shop, and a bookstore. I'd have to stop at the bookstore.

I walked up a steep hill between the bookstore and a glass-fronted jewelry store. At the top of the hill sat a large Greco-Roman marble building with four columns stretched across the front door with frescos above it. Etched in marble across the top were the words "Pawtucket Public Library". I climbed the stairs, but saw a huge steel bar across the mahogany doors.

Well, I thought, *that's a crazy library.*

I climbed back down the stairs and walked a few yards to the right side of the library. This time I saw a glass-enclosed area that looked like it had been built at least twenty years ago. Above it, in gold letters, it said *Pawtucket Public Library.* Someone carrying books came out through a set of sliding glass doors. I shrugged and headed to the door that had an up-arrow sign. The door slid open as I stood before it.

I stepped into the coolness of the library. Yes, the desk in front of me looked like it had been new twenty years ago. Now it looked abused and dated.

I turned to the right, and then right again. I entered a huge room. There were magazines against the wall. Above me was a glass-enclosed area with what looked like couches with primary-colored cushions pressed up against the glass. There were couches down here too, upholstered in burnt orange and dark green burlap. I studied the magazines, finally picking up an issue of *Time* in a clear plastic binder.

"Don't even think about stealing it," said a voice, and I froze. *No. It couldn't be.*

I turned around slowly. Seated in a dingy off-orange, graffiti-laden block chair, was a man wearing a black suit and a black tie. His trademark fedora rested on his knee, so I could see his wavy black hair. He didn't wear sunglasses, though, and the gray eyes that all Knights Templar bore as protection against demons and wizards glared at me from under hooded lids.

"Ritter," I said. "How did you find me?"

"I have my ways," he said.

He sat back in the chair. I turned to face him fully.

"I'm not stealing anything," I said. I didn't steal the clothes I wore. I'm sure the charges would show up. "It's a library. I can read the books here."

"Is this where you're going to spend your time?" he said. "In the library? They don't have the *Key of Solomon* here. I checked."

"I don't only read magic books, you know."

"You might be interested in something called *Harry Potter*. Right up your alley."

"Already read it. Before."

"And?"

"It was a joke."

"You think they don't have academies of magic? They certainly do, available to a select few. But then, you wouldn't be allowed in now."

I sighed. "What do you want, Ritter?"

He crossed his arms. "I'm watching you, Grimaulkin."

He called me by my prison name. I felt a chill. "Don't call me that."

"That's your name, isn't it? Your magical name."

"I don't go by that name out here," I said.

He gave me a smirk. "It's your name." He got up. "Just know that I'm watching you. You screw up, I'll know it."

The Templar walked past me, out of the room. I listened hard to try and hear the door close, but I was too far away.

Ritter was the one who had arrested me, who told me about Aunt Jane, and took it upon himself personally to guard me. He knew me better than anyone in that prison. He had watched me like a hawk — and would often dig his claws in like one as well. He must have heard me talking to Grimalkin the few times the demon appeared to me while in prison, because I had been sent to the prison confessor more often than any of my cellmates.

I sat down in one of the wing-back chairs and stared at the spot where Ritter had been. Grimalkin was right: the Knights knew. I had to be on my best behavior even on the outside — and keep them away from Evie and Dom. Who knew what they might say about me to Evie and Dom?

Someone peeked into the room. A young woman, her brown hair pulled up in a pony tail, smiled at me. "Everything all right, sir?"

"Yeah," I said.

She came further into the room. She looked about my age, maybe a little younger, with light skin and cornflower blue eyes behind stylish rectangular glasses. "Can I help you find anything?"

I sighed. "Inner peace."

"Oh. We have some CD's with guided meditations."

"I was kidding."

"I'm sorry." She frowned, then immediately smiled again. "If you need anything, I'm right out here. I'm Jessica."

"Thank you," I said.

She nodded and left. I sat back in the seat. Well, now that my visit here was ruined, I decided to go check out the bookstore down the street.

When I got there, imagine how my heart leapt when I saw it wasn't just a measly old used-book store. No. It was a New Age bookstore. The window was decorated with Christmas lights and hand-painted signs, advertising card readings, oracle readings, classes in "Finding your Totem Animal", and something called *Reiki*. I had heard about it in prison, but didn't know exactly what it was. I tried the door.

Locked.

I put my hand against the glass and peered inside. No one was there. The hours were posted: Wednesday, Thursday, and Friday, 11:30-7; Saturday 9-8. What day was it? I knew the date — April 20, 2000 — but not the day.

I walked up the street and finally found what I was looking for: a newspaper machine. I peered at the newspaper shoved in the glass display: Thursday.

"Good," I said. And decided to head back to the library to kill some time.

Jessica smiled when she saw me come in. I walked right up to her. "I'm sorry, but I'm new here, and was wondering if it's okay if I read in the library."

"It's what it's here for," she said, with a little giggle.

A woman behind her said, "No loitering."

This woman was short and heavy-set, with curly black and gray hair, light brown skin, and angry brown eyes. She looked me up and down, assessing whether I was homeless, I was sure.

"I swear, I'll be enriching my mind the entire time I'm here."

Again, another-up-and-down look. "Humph," she said and turned away from us.

"She always that ornery?" I asked Jessica quietly.

"A lot of homeless people come in here for the air conditioning or the heat," she said. "They scare away some patrons."

"I'll hide in a corner." I glanced at the room I had been in before, but I could tell by the books that were on the shelves that they were fiction novels. "Where's the non-fiction books?"

She pointed to the right her to a hallway that split off into a ramp and another hallway. "Up the ramp," she said. "Just keep going to the old part of the library."

Following her directions, I found myself in a large sunlit room with two floors of books on the right-hand side. The reference desk was placed before the two mahogany doors, to my left. As I approached the shelves, I could smell the welcoming scent of old books and couldn't help but grin. I romped in the stacks, taking down book after book that struck my fancy.

I hadn't realized how the time passed until my stomach started to growl. It was probably long past lunch, and the bookstore should be open now. I put the book I was reading back and left the library, giving a smile to Jessica as I walked past the check-out desk.

I almost jogged down the steep hill to the bookstore. A hand-painted "Open!" sign was on the door now, so I opened it.

A bell tinkled above my head. I smelled the patchouli immediately. Patchouli was a scent used in magic for attracting money. Underneath it was the aroma of sandalwood, used for success and protection. To my left was a section with crystals and wind chimes; on my right, shelves with candles and incense sticks, jars of resins and herbs.

The place was small, but packed. I looked at the cash register area: no one was there. The glass cases had jewelry: pentacles, runes — that is, the old-fashioned Norse Futhark runes — animals, Celtic knots.

"Be right with you, Frank," said a voice from the back.

I looked around. Did he mean me? I waited at the glass counters. Then he came out.

With red hair and pale skin, he wore only a simple green cotton vest and a necklace with a Celtic design on it, along with a tight choker of beads or shells.

About my age, I thought.

He wiped his hands on a cloth, saying, "I was just cleaning up after —" He looked up. "Oh. Hello."

I smiled at him, looking at his green eyes, not at the well-built hairless chest that the vest barely covered. "Not who you were expecting?"

"Uh, no." He chuckled. "Usually someone else comes in about this time."

"Sorry to disappoint. I was in the area, so …"

"Oh, no, stay, stay. Look around."

"Thanks," I said, and walked over to the incense. "Got any mandrake?"

"No," he said, settling into place behind the cash register.

"Wolfsbane? Belladonna?"

"I don't have anything like that."

I sighed. And here I was, excited.

"You have the simple stuff for baby pagans." I turned to face him. "*Key of Solomon?*"

"I don't have anything to do with the Left-Hand Path," he said firmly. The Left-Hand Path was what New Agers liked to call Black Magic — the magic I was familiar with and had gotten me in trouble.

"Only good magic?"

He smiled. "Baby pagan magic."

I chuckled. He was cute. I kept glancing at his chest and abs, exposed as they were for all to see.

"Been practicing long?" he asked.

"Over ten years."

He squinted his eyes as he studied me "You don't seem to be the type to go down that path."

"I did go down that path for a while. But I'm trying the straight and narrow."

He laughed, "Good luck with that. Even I can't do that."

I held out my hand. "I'm Mike."

"Scott." We shook hands. His hands were warm, but dry; a firm handshake. We sized each other up. "You have a lot of power."

"So do you," I said. He did, I could tell. While mine was darker, I'm sure, his was like spring water, flowing freely to me. I released his hand. "How did you know that?"

"I'm the 'healer' here."

The door opened, sending another tinkle of bells wafting through the air. We both looked to the entrance. A man came in wearing a brown suit and a cream-colored button-down shirt, his black tie askew. His brown hair looked as if he had just rolled out of bed. "Hey, Scott," he said, and then focused on me.

"Hi, Frank," Scott said. He motioned toward me. "This is Mike."

"Hello," I said. Frank looked me over. I could see the strap around his shoulder. He was packing heat.

"Frank's the neighborhood PI," said Scott, with a smile. "Finder of lost people, detector of wayward husbands and wives."

"Don't forget counselor of the crazy." He stepped over to the glass case. "I'm hurting for rent again."

Scott sighed. "When are you going to advertise?"

"I'm trying to get an in with the cops."

Scott said to me, "He used to be a cop in … where was it, Maryland?"

"Yeah, Maryland."

"So what happened?" I said.

"Fired."

"Oh."

"Excessive force," said Scott.

"Oh."

Frank continued, "I was drinking a lot, and this kid got in my face, so I punched him. IA fired me."

"Sorry to hear that," I said.

Frank turned to Scott. "So now that you've aired my dirty laundry to this guy, can you do some hocus-pocus to get me some customers that will actually pay me?"

"You're asking for a lot," said Scott with a smirk.

"I can," I said. They both turned to me. I grinned. "On one condition."

Frank said, "What's that?"

"I help," I said, "and get a quarter of the money."

"Why do you want to help?"

"I'm trying to do good things." I smiled over at Scott.

Frank looked like he was thinking about it. "It depends on the kind of work. If it's following some missing person, I could use the help."

"So be it," I said. "Give me something of yours so I can do the spell."

Frank looked at Scott. Scott said, "I don't know him, Frank. But I think he can do what you want."

Frank shrugged, and tucked a hand into his inside jacket pocket. I spied the gun in its holster. He pulled out a business card. "Will this do?"

I nodded. "Yep." I pocketed the card.

Of course, I couldn't do a full-blown ritual; Ritter would be on me in a heartbeat. I would have to do something like what I did with the credit card, draw a rune, and then send the request to the Universe to have it manifest. I personally disliked doing things like that; the Universe was sometimes fickle, and would make things manifest in strange and odd ways. The difference between this and the credit card was that I enforced my will on the credit card. Because I didn't know what kind of things a PI did, I would have to let the Universe decide and send him someone — or something — that would match his need.

"I'll get started on this right away," I told him. "You should be getting something in a couple of days at most."

"You got a phone number so I can call you?"

I looked around the store. "I'll stop by either here or the library."

"Frank's office is right upstairs," said Scott.

"So that's how you know each other?"

"Yes," said Frank.

"I see." I patted my pocket. "I'll come back later."

"All right," said Frank.

I looked between the two of them. Frank had his hands at his sides, and Scott was trying not to look at me directly.

"Have a good afternoon, you two," I said, heading to the entrance. I stopped and looked back at Scott, who was watching me. He smiled. So did I.

I walked back home, the idea for the spell in my mind. I had to keep it there until I actually did the work. I couldn't let it loose until I was ready.

CHAPTER FOUR

FIRST CASE

W HEN I GOT BACK TO THE APARTMENT, Rufus was happy to see me. Dom and Evie weren't home, so I retrieved the leash and took him out for a walk, still mulling the spell over and over in my mind. After the walk, I gave Rufus a treat and found a small porcelain bowl.

I walked back outside and searched around the base of the building for some loose soil. I found someone's old flower bed along the fence to the neighbor's property. With a whispered spell of gratitude to the Earth for Her gift, I scooped some soil into the porcelain bowl, then I headed back upstairs.

I opened and closed drawers until I found what I wanted: a book of matches. I took out the Flair pen from the desk. On the back of Frank's business card, I drew a Rune of Attraction combined with a Rune of Prosperity and signed it.

I couldn't call on my usual spirits — one of the seventy-two demons of Hell. I probably couldn't call on one of their corresponding angels, either.

"By my will," I said, as I lit the match. "I ask the Universe for assistance in the matter of receiving paying clients to work for." I touched the lit match to the business card; it caught instantly. The combined runes flashed purple, then disappeared in the smoke from the burning card.

I let the card burn out in the bowl of soil, all the while concentrating with my will that Frank would have lines of customers, people who needed his help and were willing to pay for it. After the card burned thoroughly, and ashes were in the bowl, I knew the spell was complete.

I ate a quick lunch, and then took the walk back to the bookstore, carrying the bowl of soil with the ashes of the card with me. When I got there, I saw a door that led upstairs from the New Age store and restaurants, so I entered the building through that door. It opened onto a set of old wooden stairs. At the landing, it led to a corridor that followed the length of the building, with doors set every ten feet or so along it. I read each of the doors. Some had names; most didn't. One door had "Frank Bennett" hand-written on a piece of paper taped on the door's frosted glass window. I knocked on that one.

"Yeah," called a voice.

I stepped inside. "Hi!"

"Oh, it's you." Bennett looked excited to see me for an instant, then he looked deflated. He wasn't wearing his jacket, so I could see the piece in his holster at his armpit.

I offered him the bowl. "Put this in the highest place, out of the way."

He took the bowl and looked inside it. "What's in it?"

"Magic," I said.

"Looks like a bowl of dirt to me, but I'll try anything at this point." He looked around. He ended up climbing on a chair and tucking it on a high shelf. "How long will it take?"

I shrugged. "Could be a couple of days, could be a week. No longer than a full turn of the moon."

He sat down. "Great, I need the rent money now."

And, as if on cue, there came a knock on the door. "Hello?"

"Yes?" Bennett stood up and a woman entered the room.

She wore a nice black dress with big white flowers on it, heels, and a light gray jacket. Behind her was a man in a suit, but he looked like he had been stuffed in it. Too tight for him, the grey charcoal suit was too light for his olive skin,

"You're the private investigator?" asked the woman.

"Yes, ma'am. Please, sit down." He looked up at the man and held out his hand. "Frank Bennett."

"Andy Blake," said the man. "My wife, Kathy."

Bennett shook hands with her. "Mrs. Blake. How can I help you?"

I stepped back, behind them, and whispered the spell of invisibility that Grimalkin taught me while I was in prison. It helped get me out of a few tight scrapes with prisoners, but the Knights could see right through the spell.

"My daughter's gone missing."

"You did report this to the police?"

Mrs. Blake nodded. "The Providence Police."

"And?"

"They said they'd look into it. She's too old for an Amber Alert, you see."

"She's over 18?"

Mrs. Blake nodded again. "She's in college. PC." I wasn't sure what college that meant. I'd have to ask later.

"How do you know she's missing?"

"Her roommate hasn't seen her for three days," said Mrs. Blake.

"It's been only three days?"

"Kelly calls us every night," Mrs. Blake answered.

Blake frowned. "The Providence Police probably said something to the effect that they can't do anything?"

"They said that it was too early for a full investigation," Mr. Blake said.

"They would say that. Even *I* would say that."

"I just know something's wrong," said Mrs. Blake. "Call it mother's intuition, but she always called us."

"Do you understand how much my services would cost?"

"We're prepared for it," Mr. Blake replied.

Mrs. Blake pulled a checkbook from her purse. "Please, anything. Kelly's our only child."

I rolled my eyes. Wow, the Universe really gave us a good one.

"It's $25 an hour," he said. "Plus mileage. And I'm cheap."

"Here's $200," Mrs. Blake said, holding out a check. "That should be enough to start?"

Frank blinked. "Do you have a picture of her?"

After taking the check, he asked them a few simple questions. Where did she like to go? Who was her roommate? Where was the dorm? Anything about her. She sounded like a girl who was still stuck on rainbows and unicorns, but even I knew that once a child was set loose from the family, their true colors came out. Maybe she drank behind their backs? Maybe she had sex with a boyfriend or two?

Her parents shook their head at those questions. No, she was a choir girl. Into the church, *etcetera.* That's why she wanted to go to Providence College, Mrs. Blake said.

"I'll make some calls," Bennett said standing up. "I'll keep you informed every step of the way."

Mrs. Blake rose. They shook hands all around, and Bennett escorted them to the door.

As soon as he hustled them out the door, I stepped forward, out of the spell. "So, where do we go first?"

He whirled around. "Jesus Christ!"

"… has nothing to do with this."

He put his hand over his heart. "Where did you come from?"

"I've been here this whole time." I said, motioning to the check, "I think out of that, you give me $50?"

"Jesus. I didn't even see you."

"Magic," I said. "So where do we go first?"

"*I* make some phone calls," he said. "I want to be sure that they, in fact, did a missing person's report and this isn't just some random member of the family trying to scoop up some tycoon's daughter."

"Better cash that check, then."

"After I make the phone calls."

I sat down in the chair that Mrs. Blake vacated. "You mundanes, always looking a gift horse in the mouth."

He glared at me, as if thinking that would make me leave. I crossed my legs and leaned back in the chair, settling in.

He got on the phone, calling someone in the Providence police department. It was legit: Kelly Dana Blake had been reported missing from Providence College by Andrew and Kathleen Blake, her parents.

Bennett turned the check over in his hands.

"Don't trust them, still?" I asked. I glanced behind me at the clock. It was quarter to five. I should head home, but this was too exciting.

"It's too coincidental."

"I tell you, it's magic — the strength and ability to change the course of events in accordance with my will."

"Scott never explained that magic worked that way."

"Because he's probably a goody —" I bit my tongue, as Bennett jerked his head up sharply. I looked down. "Sorry."

"If you're gonna help, you're not going to say one word about Scott, you got it? He's a good kid."

"I got it," I said, feeling a little sheepish.

He held up the check. "I'm going to deposit this check at the ATM. Where do you live, so I can pick you up in the morning?"

"Want to give me a ride home? It's not far from here."

He shrugged. I followed him out of his office to the bank, where he deposited the check via ATM, and then he brought me to a beat-up silver Honda Accord. It beeped when he unlocked it.

"Seen better days," I said, slipping into the passenger seat. The door didn't close when I tried to shut it.

"It runs and nobody wants it. Lift the door when you close it."

I did what he said, and the door clicked shut. I put the seatbelt on just in case. He followed my directions to the house.

"I'll be here at 7:30," he told me.

"Fine with me," I replied, and smiled at him. "Good to be doing business with you."

"Yeah." He seemed distracted, probably thinking about the case. "Now get out."

I got out of the car, closing it by lifting the door and slamming it shut. He sped off, leaving me in front of the house. I turned around to see the old woman from that morning scowling at me through a window on the first floor. I smiled and waved, and then went upstairs to the apartment.

"Mike," said Evie when I came into her view at the kitchen. Dom was sitting on the couch, watching something on TV.

"Hi, Evie," I said, and gave her a quick peck on the cheek. She stood over the frying pan, stirring some flat pieces of chicken.

"Mike, did you have anything to do with my job this morning?"

"Not intentionally. Why?"

"Because that teacher's going to be out for the rest of the school year on medical leave, and they asked me to step in for her."

"It's only a couple of months, right?"

"Until June."

"But that's good, isn't it?"

She shrugged. "I could take the bus in, or have Dom drop me off, and get a ride back home."

"I found a job," I said.

"You did?" said Dom from the couch. He got up and came over to me. "Doing what?"

"I'm helping out the local PI."

"We have a local PI?" asked Evie.

"Yeah. I went to the library, stopped at the bookstore, and the guy walked in. I offered to help him in exchange for a quarter of his take."

"Help him how?" asked Dom.

"Oh, you know. Magic."

"Mike," said Evie, narrowing her eyes at me. "You're not going to make his credit card steal stuff, are you?"

"No! It's totally on the up and up. In fact, we have our first case tomorrow." I leaned in. "A missing person."

"Who?" asked Dom.

"Kelly Blake?"

Dom shook his head. "Never heard of her."

"It sounds to me like over-concerned parents. She's probably sleeping off a drunken stupor somewhere."

"Probably." Dom didn't look convinced even as he said it, though. "You find anything, you call me, okay?"

Evie chuckled. "Always on the hunt for a story."

"I need a phone to call you," I said.

"We should pick one up for you," Evie said. "In case you're late, you can leave a message on the machine."

Rufus came up to me, smelling of dog food. He pushed his nose under my hand and I petted his head.

"I'll take him to the Cingular store tomorrow," said Dom.

"Oh, no," I said. "I'll be working! I start at 7:30."

Evie stirred pasta into a pot. "Dinner's almost done."

It was chicken and ziti with tomato sauce and fake Parmesan cheese. Among the best meals I'd ever had, it reminded me of mom, who used to make it every Wednesday night.

After dinner, we sat on the couch to watch TV, though I wasn't into it. *Friends*, then *Daddio*, and I begged off to sleep. They went into the bedroom to watch TV there, and I lay down on the couch.

I could hear them laughing at the TV, which eventually fed into a dream where I was in the Hole, a place I hadn't ended up because of my "good behavior", but was spoken about by both the Knights and the prisoners. My imagination ran wild; it was a place where the cots had nails, the concrete floors were constantly cold, and the prisoners were barefoot or even naked. I was there, in the Hole, naked as I had been before I discovered weights, and they — whoever *they* were — laughed at me. I swore, in my mind, that I would get back at them.

I stepped outside at 7:30, a half hour after Evie left with Dom, and saw the beat-up Accord parked across the street. I lifted the door open and climbed in the passenger side. Bennett set his coffee down in the cup holder between us and brushed crumbs from his chest. "Got you a coffee."

"I don't drink coffee," I said.

He raised an eyebrow at that. "Oh, all right. I can drink enough for us both." He started the car and we headed south to Providence.

"What brings you to town?" he asked me.

"My sister lives here."

"Where you from?"

"New Haven."

"New Haven not cosmopolitan enough for you?"

"You could say that."

He snorted, changing lanes. "We're going to Providence College, talk to the roommate. Let me do the talking."

"Wouldn't have it any other way."

"I'll give you the $50 when we're done today."

"Okay."

He was silent the rest of the way, probably thinking of what to ask the roommate when we saw her. (I assumed it was a *her*.)

We got to the campus, which sprawled over a few blocks. We ended up parking half way across town and hiking back to the university. I exaggerate, but that's what it felt like.

Kelly shared an apartment with four other girls on off-campus housing. As we approached the apartment, the sound blaring from either a stereo system or the TV was a dead giveaway that this was off-campus.

The girl who answered the door wore a half-shirt and shorts, "What," she said, chewing gum like a cow with cud.

"I'm here to see Vicki."

"You with the cops?"

"No."

She stepped aside and let us in. After slamming the door, she yelled out into the other room, "Hey, Vicki! Somebody ta see ya." Barefoot, she sashayed into the room with the blaring TV, picked up a remote, and turned it down.

Vicki came into the foyer where we had been left standing. She was a petite girl with wide brown eyes, and thick brown hair that cascaded just past her shoulders.

"I'm glad I caught you," said Bennett, after introducing himself. "When was the last time you saw Kelly?"

"Sunday?" She put her hand on one hip and leaned on one leg, tilting her head slightly to the right as she thought back. "Yeah. Sunday morning. She was going to the library to look up some stuff. The Internet here is slow."

Bennett asked her a series of questions. I half-listened, looking around the apartment. I already had an idea, but I needed something that belonged to Kelly. I interrupted Bennett's interrogation.

"Can I see some of her things?"

"Huh?" Vicki turned to me, as if seeing me for the first time. "Huh, yeah, sure."

She brought me to a room, the door wide open, and waved her hand to motion me inside. Bennett scowled at me for interrupting his train of thought.

I went into the room and found just what I was looking for: a hairbrush. I took some of the hair from the brush — Kelly apparently had long, fine brown hair. I saw some earrings on the bureau and took one of those as well. I had what I needed.

Bennett asked a few more questions, and then we left.

He started to head deeper into campus, but I said, "Frank?"

He turned around. "What?"

"I think I can find her faster."

"What do you mean?"

I held up the earring. "Sympathetic magic. Like finds like. Her essence is on this earring because she owned it and wore it." I unthreaded one of the fine hairs from the tangle I had grabbed off the brush. "And this is her hair. I can't get a more powerful compass than that."

"What're you going to do?" he approached me warily.

I slipped the earring onto the hair, and held the two ends between my finger and thumb. With a little force of my will, I ordered, "Come together."

The makeshift pendulum swung right to left for a moment, then a circle, then right to left again, heading right on a high arc. I turned in that direction, and the pendulum swung toward and away from me, the arc away from me much higher.

"That way."

"That's south." He watched the swinging earring. "You expect me to believe that?"

"What else were you planning on doing?"

He turned from me in disgust, heading back into the campus. I shrugged, put the pendulum in my pocket, and followed him.

He was talking to the desk clerk when I walked in. I approached as the clerk said to Bennett, "I'm sorry. I don't think I can let you see those."

"Can I speak to your manager?"

She turned away without saying anything, and headed to a back room. I leaned in toward Bennett.

"You know, my way's easier."

"Shut up," he said, waving a hand.

I stepped aside, slightly pissed off, but not enough to do anything about it. Not that I would. He was my ride home, after all.

When the clerk returned, a man a couple of years older than me followed her.

"Is there a problem?" he asked us.

"I noticed a camera at the front doors outside," said Bennett. "I'd like the see the surveillance tapes."

"What for?"

Bennett took out the picture of Kelly. It was her graduation picture. I hadn't seen it before. She wore a blue gown, her cap tilted jauntily on her head. Her eyes shone brightly in the picture, sharing some joke with the photographer. She had a nice, clear face, unlike many kids that age with zits. She looked healthy and ready to take on the world.

"Have you seen her?"

They both shook their heads. "No," said the manager. "Is she missing?"

"Yes."

"Are you with the police?"

"No."

"Then, I'm sorry. We can't help you."

Bennett frowned, tucking the picture back in his jacket. "Mind if I ask some people?"

"Yes, we do mind."

"Okay," said Bennett and he walked out of the library. I jumped to follow him.

Bennett stood outside and asked people who came into the library whether any of them had seen Kelly. We did this until campus security kicked us out.

As we walked back to the car, I checked the pendulum. Always heading south.

"Frank?"

"What?" he snapped, walking a little ahead of me.

"Can we *please* try my way?"

He stopped walking and turned to face me. "Look. If it's pointing the way it's going, it's more than likely that she's been kidnapped."

"Kidnapped?" I asked. How did he know?

"Call it detective intuition, but she didn't head home, which is north, and didn't head back to campus. She went off campus with someone she knew."

"But not a stranger?"

"Most people are not kidnapped by strangers."

I knew of a few kidnappers in prison. I never really found out their motives, but if they were there for heinous crimes like mine, their motives must not have been good.

"Do we go back to Vicki?"

"I wish I could see the tape. Then I'd know she left with someone."

"I can't help with that," I said, even as I heard Grimalkin immediately whisper in my ear.

"Yes, you can."

I turned around to see him standing behind me. "Okay," I asked him. "How?"

"Huh?" asked Bennett.

"Go back. Lie. They will believe."

"No," I said, and turned back to Bennett, who was looking at me like I was crazy. "Sorry." I walked past him, heading to the car.

We got in the car and Bennett sat back. "So. We head south?"

"Yes," I said.

We started threading through the streets, ending up in downtown Providence before I said, "Take the highway."

"How far did she go?" he asked, when we got to Warwick.

At that point, the pendulum swung in a southwesterly direction.

"This exit," I said.

He crossed two lanes of traffic to get off the highway. We ended up going down residential streets, while the pendulum swung toward the southwest, and then north. We found that we were driving around a small park. A very small section of trees and a baseball field sat to the side of the trees and a playground close to that.

He pulled into in the parking lot next to the baseball field. The pendulum swung wildly toward the trees.

"Shit," said Bennett, and he held out a hand to stop me from heading into the small copse of trees. "Are you sure that thing's accurate?"

"In theory, it should be."

"Shit," he said again. He took out his flip phone. "Yes. West Warwick, Rhode Island police. Not 911." He told them where we were, and asked for a patrol car to come down. "There's a missing person and this was the last place she was believed to have been near," he said, the white lie coming to him easily.

I stuffed the pendulum in my pocket. He hung up the phone and said to me, "Don't move. Don't even breathe in that direction," he motioned toward the trees.

"Why?"

"She's in there," he said. "According to what your swinging thing shows, right?"

"Well, yes."

"Does the other person have to be alive?"

I could now see where he was going with this.

"No," I said quietly.

A few minutes later, a patrol car arrived. Bennett nodded to the cop as if they were old friends. I stood back with the invisibility spell cloaked over me.

"I didn't want to go in there, in case," I heard Bennett tell the cop.

The cop called for another cruiser. After they arrived, the four cops went into the knot of trees, hands on their guns. I was very glad I stayed in the car.

"Jerry," called one of the cops. "Over here."

Bennett hung his head. "Shit."

A cop came out of the trees, almost running over to the cruiser, talking into his shoulder radio. "Jane Doe found dead in Jefferson Memorial Park."

Bennett waited until the cop got the response, then brought over the picture. The cop nodded, and spoke into his mouthpiece, "Correction; her name is Kelly Dana Blake. Out of PC …"

Things happened quickly after that. Bennett was whisked away and I stayed in the car. Though a couple of people looked right at me, they didn't approach. It wasn't until long after two o'clock before Bennett returned to me and his car. By then, I had to take a piss and was starving.

"Where the Hell have you been?" I said, shifting uncomfortably in the seat while he glanced at me.

"Overactive bladder?" he asked, giving me a smirk.

"I'm not used to waiting around with no place to go. What happened?"

"I had to conveniently forget how I knew Kelly was here," he said, getting into the car. "And I had to call the Blakes."

"Oh." I looked out the window. A hearse had left with the body in a big green plastic bag. I had sat and watched it all. "So now what?"

"I'll get you your fifty bucks," he said calmly.

We drove into the center of Warwick and, after driving to a McDonald's so I could relieve myself, he drove up to a bank.

He took out some money from a machine, then handed me three twenties.

"Don't worry about the change," he said. "You earned it."

I smiled. "Thanks." I pocketed the money.

"Do me a favor?" Bennet asked me flatly, as he pulled out of the bank.

"What's that?"

"Don't send any more business like that my way."

CHAPTER FIVE

DOWNTIME

THAT NIGHT, the discovery of the body was on the news. Dom was beside himself.

"Why didn't you call me?"

"Dom, I don't have a phone."

He frowned, scowled, then crossed his arms.

"You can use the money you got from work to buy a phone," said Evie. "They have free ones if you sign up for a two-year contract."

"I have to make an ID," I said.

"Make one?"

"How else am I supposed to get an ID?"

"Uh, legally?"

"Do you realize what I have to do? I'll need a birth certificate. That means going back home." I sipped some Kool-Aid that Evie made. "I'm trying to avoid that."

"I know, Mikey, but everything you've done here since you got out of that prison has been questionably legal."

"You don't have to go home," Dom pointed out. "You go to the city that your mother was living when you were born."

"New Haven? And how am I going to get there? Fly?"

They stared at me, as if expecting me to answer my own question. So I did.

"I can fly, but not that far."

"You can fly?" asked Evie in disbelief.

"Levitate, more like. Not fly." I waved a hand, dismissing the question. "It doesn't matter. I have to get there."

"I'll bring you on Tuesday," said Dom. "It's only, what, two hours?"

"Something like that. Not Monday?"

"It's a busy news day on Monday."

"Okay, Tuesday. But what address do I use?"

"This one," said Evie. "You can always change it later."

"He needs something to come in the mail with his name on it, though," said Dom

"Can't he send himself a letter?"

"No, it has to be official. Like a utility bill or something."

There came a knock on the door. All of us looked at each other in turn.

"I'm not expecting anyone," said Evie, as Dom got up.

He threaded his way around the couch to the door and opened it. "Hi, Mr. Fernandes," said Dom.

Evie leaned over to me. "Our landlord. He lives downstairs."

"You got somebody living here with you?" he said, his voice heavily accented.

I got up. Evie got up too.

Dom said, "It's Evelyn's brother."

"He can stay this week, but after that, you pay extra fifty dollars a week." He looked around Dom. He was a small man, balding, with a pot belly hanging over his belt. He wore a blue button-down mechanic's shirt, dark blue pants, and greasy work boots. "There's no room in the apartment for him."

"I'm not staying," I said. "Just need some crash space."

He looked me over. I used to get those looks in prison. It was a combination of disgust and fear, and usually meant that I would be able to win a fight. I didn't fight. I used my words to get out of it.

"I just got into town from Greece." I smiled. "I'm looking for an apartment. Got any for rent?"

"You got a job?"

"Not yet."

"When you get a job, you come see me. I get you an apartment."

"Sounds good."

Fernandes looked up at Dom, nodded to him, and then turned around, going back down the stairs. Dom closed the door and leaned against it.

"Some woman kept staring at me whenever I left," I said. "Must be his wife."

Evie nodded. "She's very nosy."

Dom said, "Were you serious about asking about an apartment? You'd probably get a closet with a hot plate for a hundred bucks a week."

"No, of course not." I sat back down on the couch. "But I'm not going to live here forever, either."

"At least until after the honeymoon," said Evie.

Dom looked pained.

"Somebody has to babysit Rufus while we go to the Bahamas."

"I'll try and get an apartment before your wedding," I said. "And babysit Rufus."

"So, it's a Friday night, and we've got some extra money," Dom said. "Want to go out?"

"Out where?" asked Evie, a tinge of caution in her voice.

Dom smiled. "PJ's? Shoot some pool?"

Evie looked like she was on the fence. I said, "That sounds like a great idea!"

Then Evie sighed. "Why do I let you talk me into everything?"

The bar was within walking distance, just a block or so away. The air was cool enough for a light jacket, but only Evie had a hoodie. I realized that I would need to get a jacket at some point. Dom and Evie walked side by side, his arm around her shoulders, with me taking up the rear.

"Remember Uncle Joey, when he would let us play pool downstairs in his house?" asked Evie.

"I remember," I said. The last time I'd seen Uncle Joey was on my 10th birthday. My parents threw a party that year. I was going to have another party on my 13th birthday, but things didn't work out that way. "How is he?"

"He got remarried again. He's coming to the wedding."

We turned a corner. There was a bar with the sign "PJ's" in green script hanging above the door. Dom held the door open for Evie and me.

We walked into a cloud of smoke. I coughed. One thing I didn't learn in prison was how to smoke. The place wasn't crowded, but it was bustling. The music was loud and heavy. Evie leaned into me and said loudly, "Pool tables are over there." She pointed. I could hardly see them for the press of people.

"What do you want?" Dom asked me.

I could only imagine what alcohol would do to me, and I really didn't want to know. One of the things drilled into me in prison was to avoid alcohol in case you needed to come up with a spell on the fly. If you were addled by alcohol or drugs, the spell would screw up, and you'd be eaten by a demon — or worse.

"Diet Coke."

"I'll take a beer," Evie said.

We threaded our way through the crowd, aiming for the pool tables. All three of them were taken. Evie sat down at a table near them, while I stood against the wall.

Dom arrived with a bottle of Coke for me. "They didn't have diet," he said.

I shrugged and took it. The sugar and caffeine would keep me awake, no doubt. Evie took her frothy beer, and Dom sipped his.

"You gonna cheat?" he asked me, grinning.

"You mean use a spell? Depends. How good are you?"

"I suck."

"Then no."

He laughed. The guy at the middle table defeated someone, and looked like he was ready to take on any comers. Dom glanced at me; I shook my head. It would be obvious, me drawing something on the pool cue. The guy was looking at us. He beckoned.

"I'll do it," Evie said, and got up.

She walked over and picked up the cue. The guy gave her an amused smirk, and racked up the balls. He let her break. She sunk a low ball.

"Hustler," whispered Dom in my ear.

"No way," I whispered back. Since when did she play pool better than both of us?

He nodded and his attention was back on his fiancé, who proceeded to clean up the table. The loser laughed, shook her hand, and left the pool cue on the table.

"Dayum," I said.

"See why I suck?"

Evie beckoned us over. We played a couple of rounds, and she proceeded to beat the pants off the both of us. I hadn't played since I was 12, and I think I sunk two balls during the entire night.

We walked back to the apartment at around midnight, and I collapsed on the couch, fully dressed, smelling like bar.

Evie chased me out of the house at 10 a.m. because she wanted to clean. She cleaned like my mother. Get the Hell out of her way, because she would run you over with the vacuum cleaner. Dom and I got the hint and decided that this was the ideal time to see if I could get a phone.

The Cingular store had just flipped its sign from Closed to Open when we arrived, and we were the first customers. The kid — he must've been about my age — let us in. "Hi, how can I help you this morning?"

"My friend needs a phone," said Dom.

"Sure." He motioned to the wall. "Pick one out."

"It can't be that easy," I said to Dom, as we walked over to the wall.

"Get one that doesn't cost anything." He pointed to a flip phone. "This is the one Evie has."

"What about this one?" I pulled up one that didn't have a flip. Instead, it had a screen with its keyboard exposed: a Nokia.

"What if you sit on it? You'll break the keys."

"Hm, yeah. I guess I'll take one like Evie has."

"Good man," said Dom. He motioned to the kid, who bounded over.

"That's our best seller," he said. "Very durable."

I held it in my hand. It seemed so small. I used my thumb and flipped it open. It kind of looked like the phone that Ashleigh had let me borrow.

"Do you have any ID?"

"No," I said.

"I do," said Dom. "I'll buy it."

"You don't have to do that."

"You promise to call me when things happen this time?"

I laughed. "Yes, I promise."

So now I was connected to the 21st century.

I found out the name of the New Age bookstore that Scott owned: *The White Raven*. Armed with my new device, I took a walk to the store.

Scott smiled when I entered. It was empty at the moment.

"Hi," he said. This time he wore a red shirt, tight against his frame.

"Hey. Look!" I showed him my phone.

He smiled. "What's your phone number?"

"Um …" I stared at the phone, not comprehending how I would even find out what my number was.

"Let me see it." He took the phone from me, and found the menu that had my phone number. As he copied down the number, he said, "I heard about how you helped Frank."

"I think I put him in a tough position," I said. "He had to explain to the cops how he knew she was there."

"I'm sure Frank can get himself out of situations like that." He leaned back, against the wall.

"I take it you two were …" I waved my hand.

"No!" he said, and his face turned the color of his shirt. Damn, he looked cute when he blushed.

"Oh. Oh, I thought —"

"We're just friends."

"I'm sorry."

His blush faded as he shrugged. "It's all right. It took a while for Frank to not feel uncomfortable around me."

I nodded. Straight guys were like that.

"Do you have anyone now?"

"No."

We both looked at each other, sizing each other up. My t-shirt wasn't as tight as his, but I'm sure he could see what I had in my jeans. "Maybe —"

He almost said something, but then the door opened and two women stepped inside.

"Ooh, it smells nice in here!" one said. The other one wrinkled her nose.

I stepped aside and pretended to look at some herbs on the wall.

After they left, other people came in. Then it became a steady stream of people. I read the sign the Universe was giving me. Threading my way out of the crowded store, I headed back to Evie's place.

CHAPTER SIX

WEEKEND

When I got back to Evie's apartment, Dom was on the computer. Evie had papers all spread out all over the kitchen counter where we ate, doing something for her teaching assignment. The stereo was playing "Layla" by Eric Clapton.

Rufus greeted me at the door. I took down his leash and he was even happier to see me. Without saying a word to either Evie or Dom, I took the dog out for a walk. I needed something else for exercise other than walking. I needed weights to do my old workout from prison. If there was anything I had learned, it was that lifting weights helped keep the pounds off.

I took Rufus to a park about the size of a small house lot. I read the plaque posted there. A major Indian fight had happened at that very spot. The plaque had been installed in 1937.

I walked Rufus toward some bushes other dogs had been using for their bathroom. As he did his duty, I looked above the bushes to see Grimalkin standing on the other side.

"Now you taste freedom," he said. "What about payment?"

"We never agreed on any 'payment'."

"Let us agree now. You have freedom. Return me to Hell."

"A banishing is just as bad as a summoning. It makes me look like I did a summoning without anyone knowing."

"You did."

I did. In the prison. Grimalkin was somehow able to get past the magical wards into prison with me.

"I guided you," he said.

It was true. He taught me spells that helped me survive in the prison. He exposed me to wizards and witches who taught me their spells in secret. While learning to box, I learned the motions for generating *chi*. While lifting weights, I learned the chant necessary for protection, and how to repel a hex. I learned a lot of things that way, and Grimalkin practiced them with me.

Rufus tugged at the leash. "I'll see what I can do," I told Grimalkin. "I have to get the implements without Ritter knowing." I turned away from him and Rufus and I walked back to the apartment.

The landlady was visible through the window downstairs, rocking back and forth in a chair, knitting or crocheting or doing something that caused her to look down at her hands and not at me.

I went upstairs and let Rufus loose in the apartment. Dom noticed me first.

"Oh, hey, Mike."

"Hey. Is there a YMCA near here?"

"Yeah. Across the street from the library."

How convenient, I thought. "Can we go there?"

"Today?"

"Yeah."

Dom shrugged. "Sure, why not. Need a ride?"

I smiled. "That was kind of the point."

Dom walked over to Evie and put his hand on her back. "Be right back, hon."

"Okay," she said, not looking up from her papers.

We went out to the car. "I should get a membership," Dom said.

"I have some money if you want to go in with me on it."

He shrugged. "I have to talk it over with Evie. You know, money's kind of tight."

The Y was exactly where Dom said, across the street from the library. It was a big four-story brick building that seemed a perfect complement to the white marble library. There was a faded blue sign above the door, but it was small and I hadn't noticed it, being that my focus had been on the library or the bookstore. We had to park down a side street because there were so many cars parked near the Y itself.

"I think they have an indoor pool," said Dom, as he parked the car.

"That's something I didn't have." I got out.

We went to the front entrance. It was open. It smelled like rotten smoke and leather, which was probably due to the creased and worn leather couches in the front lobby. A pair of men were playing cards across a small table. A pair of stairs flanked the reception desk, two up and two down. No one was at the reception desk, however, so we peeked into the office next to it.

"Hello?" I called.

"Yeah!" a woman called from a back room. She rolled her chair to the doorway and looked out at me. She appeared to be a petite woman, with black hair and a round face. "Can I help you?"

"I'd like to see your gym."

"Oh, sure. One sec, let me get someone." She rolled back out of view and, in seconds, I heard over the intercom, "Mary to the main office. Mary to the main office."

Minutes later, an older woman with gray hair cut in a bob, wearing a white shirt that had a big blue "Y" on the front, showed up. "Hello! Can I help you?"

"I'd like to see your gym."

"Sure! Thinking of becoming a member?"

"Yes."

She looked at the two of us. "Okay, come with me." We started walking down the stairs. "If you want to be members, it's $75 a year. You would have access to the gym, the pool, the locker room and you get to have a locker, but you have to stake it out with your own lock and tell us the number."

We hugged the wall as a family came up the stairs, their hair wet. They smiled and waved at us, so we waved back. We went down three floors before reaching the end of the stairway.

Mary continued. "So we're going to have a sauna near the pool, but that's being built. And you get a twenty percent discount on any classes."

We walked down a linoleum-lined corridor. I could smell the chlorine down here, so the pool was nearby. She pushed open a door and we entered a room that smelled of old sweat and mold.

The gym was small, but had what I needed and more: a rowing machine, two treadmills, three weight benches, and some other machines that I had no idea what they were used for.

"I have sixty dollars right now," I said.

"I've got ten," said Dom, pulling out his wallet.

Mary waved a hand. "Don't worry about the five dollars. I just need to see your ID."

"I don't have one yet."

"Okay, that's not a problem. Come out front, I'll get you signed up."

She continued to explain the rules, which were mostly common sense. They were going to be open on Sundays after Memorial Day.

"And if you want, you can go to the barbecue we're having outside in the courtyard."

"Barbecue?" asked Dom.

Mary handed me a membership card. She wrote my name in old-fashioned cursive, giving it a homey touch. "All you can eat hot dogs and burgers."

We looked at each other. I hadn't eaten, and I'm sure Dom could go for some burgers. We followed Mary down one level, then out to a concrete-lined courtyard that seemed the size of a postage stamp.

There were kids running around everywhere, people laughing and drinking, eating and talking among themselves. We got a hot dog, some potato salad, meatballs, and all sorts of other food out of crock pots. We stood around awkwardly for a few minutes.

"Dominic Marcello?"

Dom turned. "Hey!" He put down his plate and shook hands with a dark-skinned man who stood a good head and shoulders taller than Dom did. The man pulled him into a hug. "How the Hell are you, Javon?"

The man grinned. "Can't complain, but what good would it be? What're you doing here?"

Dom thumbed at me. "My soon-to-be brother-in-law just signed up."

Javon held his hand out to me. "Javon Martin."

"Mike LeBonte." I shook his hand, while I balanced the plate with my other hand.

"Soon-to-be brother-in-law, huh? Finally tying the knot?"

"Yeah. Met this wonderful girl that was too good to possibly lose."

"I hear ya, I hear ya. My wife's around here somewhere, along with my two little ones." He looked around briefly, then back at Dom. "So what have you been up to?"

"Not much. Trying to find a job."

"Really? What kind of job?"

"Writing. I went to school for journalism."

He tilted his head. "Would you be interested in marketing?"

"I don't know. That's copywriting, right?"

"A little of that. I'm the director here at the Y, and I could use someone to help write the newsletter."

"For pay?"

"Of course for pay. It'd be part-time. Three days a week, probably less than that. Free membership."

Dom looked like he was thinking, but he probably was ready to jump at the opportunity. "Yeah," he said finally. "I'm interested."

"That's great! Oh, here's my wife —"

A pale-skinned woman came out of the crowd. She wore a pinched look, not as open as Javon's was. She looked like she didn't want to be there among the masses of people.

"Michelle," Javon called, and the woman picked her way through the throng, avoiding touching other people. "Michelle. This is Dominic Marcello. We went to school together in Providence."

She looked down her nose at him. "Hello," she said, without offering her hand.

"And his brother-in-law, Mike."

She did the same thing with me. "Hello."

"Hi," I said.

Her mouth twitched and she turned away. "I am going inside."

"Of course, dear. Where's Lashonda and Qiana?"

Michelle motioned to the gaggle of children playing. Then she hustled into the building, as if she couldn't get out of there fast enough. Javon smiled. "She doesn't like parties much."

"I thought it was me," said Dom, looking down at himself. "I know I'm not dressed for it."

Javon put a comradely arm around Dom's shoulder. "Don't worry about it. Let me introduce you to some of the staff."

I stepped aside. I people-watched and ate, while Dom got whisked around the room.

Javon returned Dom to me after almost an hour. "You should bring your fiancé," Javon told him.

"I will next time," said Dom. "I really should be going, though." He looked at me strangely, as if I had done something wrong. I just smiled and shook Javon's hand, thanking him for the food and telling him I would see him around.

We walked back to the car, and Dom said, "Mike? Did you —"

"Did I what?"

"Did you get me that job?"

"I didn't do it intentionally."

Dom got in the car, shaking his head. "Then you are one lucky man, Mike."

The next morning, Evie told me that she had a surprise for me. I was leery of surprises. Whenever someone in the prison said they had a surprise, it never boded well.

We packed a small cooler with peanut butter and jelly sandwiches — the only thing left in the house that was transportable — and headed north on the highway. I sat cramped in the back seat because it was a two-door car. Dom drove, and seemed to know exactly where he was going

I followed the signs for a while, and finally got to a point where I was lost. It wasn't until I saw a town's sign that I had an inkling of where we were going.

The sign was black with silver lettering: "Welcome to Salem."

The witches and wizards of the prison always talked about the Mecca of our kind. This was the place where the Left-Hand Path met and worked with the New Agers. You could find everything you ever needed; you just had to ask the right people. I sat up, excited.

Evie turned around and smiled at me. "I thought you might want to look around," she said.

I kicked myself for spending my money at the Y.

We parked on the main street, and they didn't bother putting money in the parking meter. I pointed that out, but Dom said, "It's Sunday. They don't ticket on Sundays."

I looked around. It looked initially like any other New England downtown, with brick buildings and wooden storefronts. That was, until you examined the stores themselves.

Every business had to do with witchcraft, even the pet store. Pentacles, moons, and suns were everywhere. I felt like I had come home.

"Pick up your jaw," Dom said, "and let's walk around."

We started down the main street. Placards advertised more magic stores down side streets. I wanted to go into every one of them.

I came upon a store called *Spellworks*, painted black with gold trim on the edges of the building. I looked in the window, and could see candles, herbs, and implements of ritual. I looked above the threshold and saw the rune for "Buy". Unlike Scott, who had a rune of protection (a passive rune), this one was aggressive, pushy, and I felt its power as I stepped inside the store. I made a motion with my hand to dispel the rune. When Evie and Dom crossed the threshold, I put my hand on each of their shoulders and traced a rune with my finger on each of their shoulders against the demand. Both of them seemed to relax.

"What was that?" asked Dom.

I put a finger to my lips. "Shh. Explain later."

We walked around the store, no longer feeling that I had to buy something in order to leave. The entire place was decorated in black and gold. All of the items had black and gold labels on them. It seemed very gothic. The clerk was even dressed like she was gothic, with a blue velvet corset and long, flowing skirt. She was looking me over, watching me as I studied the herbs and incense, while I ignored the fact that I should be picking something up to purchase.

"Mike," said Evie, pointing to a black candle that was shaped like a woman. "What's this for?"

"Lots of things," I said. Next to it was an anatomically correct candle of a man. "You could use it for sympathetic magic."

"What's that?"

"Like attracts like," I said. I picked up the male candle. "Imagine this was a symbol of your worst enemy. You could stick pins in it to cause your enemy pain."

"Like voodoo," said Dom.

"Very like. Voodoo relies on sympathetic magic. You can also use it to heal." I touched the wick. "Or use it for eliminating some things that could be bothering you."

Evie asked, "How do you do that?"

"You put whatever is bothering you inside the candle. "

"How?"

"You feel the feeling, and then kind of send it into the candle. You push emotions outward to something else."

Evie frowned. I'd lost her somewhere. Something that came so naturally to me was something foreign to her. She moved on; I stayed with her.

"Oh, look," she said. "Cards like you used to have."

My heart leapt. A Rider-Waite tarot deck sat there on the shelf. I missed those cards. She picked them up, held the box in her hand. I could tell she was debating whether to buy them. She had the money on the credit card, so that wasn't a worry.

"Amazon might be cheaper," said Dom.

"True," she said, and put the cards back. I felt let down.

Just as I was going to ask her to buy them anyway, the front door opened. A man entered, wearing 19th century clothes: a jacket, vest, even a top hat and cane. Surveying the room, he smiled, revealing a mouth full of white teeth, a Teddy Roosevelt grin.

"Greetings!"

He sauntered over to us, the only customers in the shop.

The hackles on the back of my neck went up. Something was definitely wrong with this guy, and it wasn't just his clothes. He was a wizard — and he oozed power. Unlike the people in prison, he didn't hold his power in check. This was something I wasn't familiar with, so I closed my eyes for a moment to get my bearings, to build up my own aura against this man. Somehow, I would have to encompass Evie and Dom with it, or they could be forced to do whatever the man asked them. I put my hand on each of their shoulders while I stood behind them.

"Is there anything special you're looking for?"

Both Dom and Evie turned to me. The man focused his entire being on me, and I felt him push against my aura. He was trying to sense me … the bastard. That was something that was just not done in wizarding circles. It was like trying to invade someone's personal space. Fights happened because of that.

"Mandrake," I said.

His grin faded, just a little bit. "Whole?"

"Preferably."

"Do you know what that's used for?" he asked.

Patronizing little shit, I thought. "Yes."

He looked at Dom and Evie. I still had my hand on their shoulders. He wasn't going to get them to do what he wanted, I would make sure of that.

He looked at me, his grin gone. "I have some in the back. It will be expensive."

"How much?"

"Twenty dollars a gram."

"What is that stuff, gold?" Dom asked in a sarcastic tone.

The man chuckled. "It is a very rare herb, used for the darkest of dark magic."

"Not always," I said.

Evie said, "Mike …"

"I was just asking if he had it. I'm not planning on buying it."

"It may be easier," said the man, "and cheaper for you, if you plan on performing such black magic, if you use some of my prepared incenses that I have over here." He motioned to the left of us, toward a wall of incense in glass vials.

"I'd rather prepare it myself."

"You don't trust the Warlock of Salem?"

I raised an eyebrow. "Warlock? Are you kidding me?"

The man inclined his head. "Sebastian D'Luna, proprietor of this establishment."

"Well, Mr. D'Luna, in answer to your question: No, I don't trust the 'Warlock of Salem'."

Evie and Dom stood between us, and they both looked like they wanted to be somewhere else.

D'Luna narrowed his eyes. "You seem rather young."

"Trust me," I said firmly, "I've been in training for quite some time."

Dom pointed to the wall on his right. "Evie, come see this," he said.

They stepped out from under my hand, leaving me to face D'Luna alone, and leaving them unprotected from him. I had to keep D'Luna occupied.

It didn't take much to get him to pay attention to me. D'Luna tried to pierce the aura again. He did it so obviously, this time stepping forward into my personal space.

I backed up. "In the first place," I said. "There's no such thing as a 'warlock'."

"I'm trying to take back the name. It's what most of the … people expect."

"You mean mundanes."

"I don't use that term," he said, glancing at Evie and Dom, who were finding their way out the door. "Especially when they're expected to be my customers."

"You sell these things to normal people?"

"Of course." Again, that Teddy Roosevelt grin. "I give them instructions and sell them whatever they need for whatever spell they wish to do."

I watched Evie and Dom walk out. Did the Rosicrucians know about this? Because if this man sold to mundanes, I was surprised he was still in business.

The Rosicrucians would not tolerate a wizard — or whatever he called himself — teaching a mundane how to do black magic. Some of the stuff in this store was for the serious practitioner, like me, but the pre-packaged items were for the ones who wanted the quickest way to get results. If a mundane bought one of his "prepared spells", that was akin to providing them with the tools for the magic the Rosicrucians protected against, not to mention that the user may end up in prison.

"What if the spell backfires?"

He laughed. "Spells don't 'backfire.' They just don't work. It's entirely the intent of the caster." He gazed at me. "If you were in training for as long as you say you were, you would have known that."

I got in his face. "Don't patronize me."

He didn't back off. In prison, this would have meant a fight. "You were a mundane once, too."

"Maybe for the first few years of my life," I said. "But I learned fast." I pushed by him and headed toward the door.

He laughed at me.

I whirled around. Part of me was screaming, *Never attack a witch in his own home.* But I noticed one thing about this building: there was nothing about protection. It was all "Buy. Buy. Buy."

"Expect a visit from the Rosicrucians."

Now his grin faded. "Why?"

I grinned. "They're watching me." I motioned around the store. "You sell items to mundanes for the Left-Hand Path. They're not going to like that."

"It's up to the caster," he said, as I shut the door on him.

The Rosicrucians, the Knights Templar, wouldn't take that as an excuse. They had arrested me because I was following the Left-Hand Path, the path of dark and evil magic. Oh, and probably because I killed few people in town through the use of Belial. The deaths were secondary to the Rosicrucians, though.

I caught up with Evie and Dom at an art gallery two doors down. "Sorry," I said.

"That guy was creepy," said Evie.

I nodded. "Some wizards create the creepy persona," I said to her. "It keeps people away from them."

There were a few other stores, all of them with the *Buy* rune over the threshold. I kept guiding them away from the magic stores, though Evie looked confused each time. Finally, we got to the end of a pier, with a clam shack that was closed for the season. Evie turned around to me.

"Why don't you want to go into those stores?"

"Because they all have a spell on them." I looked at Dom. "Didn't you feel like you needed to buy something in that creepy store?"

"Well, yeah," said Dom. "I thought it was just because, well, you're into it and …"

"No," I said firmly. "No. Don't get into it, Dom."

"We're trying to be supportive," said Evie, putting a hand on one hip.

"I love you for that, Evie," I said, putting my hand on her arm. "But, really, you guys, I don't want you involved in magic."

She frowned. "We came here for nothing, then?"

"Not unless you plan on buying that tarot deck."

"Not from that creepy guy."

I laughed. "No. Not from that creepy guy."

We went to a few stores, but I could tell Evie was creeped out by some of the items, or by the people behind the counter. I suspect the rune I drew on their shoulders was still active, and made her sensitive to the pushy runes on the threshold. She never did buy the cards for me. Which, in a way, I was glad for, because I didn't want to feel guilty whenever I used them.

The next day, I went to the Y for my first exposure to their gym. The equipment was in excellent condition and worked fine. I had the place to myself. I used the treadmill and ran for a 3/4 mile, five times around the full circuit of the exercise yard. I lifted, did crunches, sit-ups, pull-ups, and tried the rowing machine. Then I took a quick shower.

After that, I went to library. I didn't see the sign "No Cell Phone Use In The Library" until it was too late. Even if I had seen the sign, I wouldn't have known how to shut the phone off. Luckily, I was in the back of the stacks, perusing a book on ancient Egyptian goddesses, when it went off.

The noise made me jump. I fumbled as I pulled out the phone and flipped it open.

"Hello?" I whispered, looking around and hoping nobody noticed.

"Mike," said Bennett. "Meet me at the office in five minutes."

He must have gotten my number from Scott.

"You're lucky I'm not home," I said, but he already hung up. If I was home, I couldn't get to his place in five minutes. I put the book back — I still remembered the Dewey decimal system — and that's when I saw the sign about cell phones. Hopefully, nobody had noticed.

I half-snuck out of the library and walked down the hill to Bennett's office.

He stood outside in the doorway to the stairs leading to the second floor. "C'mon," he said, and brought me to his car.

"Where are we going?"

"Slater Park."

"For what?"

"Something that's right up your alley."

I settled in for the ride, which was full of traffic.

When we got there, he parked right on a dirt path, and then we walked to a section that was marked off in police tape. He stopped in front of a cop and told him, "Detective Hotchkiss called us."

The cop nodded and lifted the tape for us. There were a dozen or so cops walking around, looking at the ground, as we headed toward a circle of trees set between two meadows.

I felt it before I saw it. It made my hair on the back of my neck stand up on end: the remnant of a wild spell set loose.

Bennett walked up to a tall, thin man with small shoulders. He wore a loose black and blue striped tie over a charcoal shirt, covered by a form-fitting jacket of a slightly darker shade of charcoal. He wore black pants and loafers. His face was thin and angular like he was, pinched at the jaw, a tight oval. His eyes were too big for his face, though.

"Frank," said the man, giving him an upnod. "Is this the magician?"

"Yes," said Frank. "Mike, meet Detective Aaron Hotchkiss."

"Sir," I said, shaking his hand. "What can I do for you?"

He motioned behind me. At first, I didn't see what he was gesturing toward because the grass was so high here. Then I noticed part of the grass had been ripped out and tossed aside. I walked closer, then squatted down.

The grass had been torn up by the roots in a two-foot radius. In the center was a badly drawn sigil in black. A brush rested next to the sigil.

I knew that sigil from sight.

"All right," came a voice coming from behind me, "I'm here."

I hunched my shoulders. *Son of a bitch,* I thought, and turned around to see Sebastian D'Luna, still dressed in his damn nineteenth-century clothes, even including the cape. He swirled it from his shoulders and handed it to a sycophant. She looked pale, dressed head to toe in black velvet and lace, including dark velvet gloves.

I rolled my eyes and rose from my crouch. He saw me.

"What is *he* doing here?"

"I thought I'd get a second opinion," said Hotchkiss.

D'Luna snorted, ignoring the jibe, and strode over to where I was standing. He looked down at the ground, then at the sigil. I didn't see any recognition cross his face. He sniffed, raised his head, and said, "Your perpetrator is in South Providence."

Hotchkiss turned to an Hispanic man in a suit, who shrugged his shoulders. "Thanks," said Hotchkiss and turned to me. He nodded upward to me — a signal, I guess, for me to speak.

"Whoever did this," I told him, "botched it."

Hotchkiss tilted his head. "What do you mean?"

"This is a sigil to summon a demon," I explained. "When you summon a demon, you're supposed to be in a protective circle, and you're supposed to have a containment circle around the demon. He tried to make a circle." I pushed aside some of the grass. "But he didn't even try to make a containment circle with salt."

D'Luna sniffed. "I don't think the detective cares about that."

"Shut up," Hotchkiss told him. "Go on," he said, turning back to me. Bennett's face held a touch of a smirk.

"He might have made a protective circle by just pushing down the grass," I continued. "But you probably can't tell now with everyone walking around. Or he really was stupid enough to just draw the sigil and start the invocation without any protections."

"What happens if you don't have protection?" asked the other guy in the suit.

D'Luna answered. "You lose control of what you try to invoke."

"What's that mean?"

I waited for D'Luna. He just shrugged his shoulders.

"It could mean a few things," I said. "The demon is set loose in the world. However, the higher up you go on the food chain, the harder it is for that particular demon to stay in the world, so it has to usually possess someone."

"And what demon is this? Do you know?"

I nodded, glancing back at the sigil. "Belial."

D'Luna squared his shoulders. He looked ready to launch into a pedantic rant.

"Who's Belial?" Hotchkiss asked, cutting him off.

"Third to Lucifer. This is the simple sigil," I told Hotchkiss, not looking at D'Luna. "His full seal is a lot more complicated. But yeah, this is Belial's sigil."

"It's not *really* Belial, of course," D'Luna said. "It's a spirit that embodies what Belial endows."

This guy was full of it. I opened my mouth to tell him so, when he turned to me, fury on his face. "You are attempting to scare these poor people into thinking the Devil possessed someone."

"It's true."

The guy next to Hotchkiss said, "Wait, the Devil has possessed someone?"

"More than likely," I said. "And that person won't last long. You get possessed, it eats you up from the inside."

"That is all theory, of course," said D'Luna.

He was talking out of his butt. I wanted to ask him if he ever summoned a demon, but I kept it civil.

"How do you know all this?" asked the Hispanic guy that I didn't know.

"I studied it for about ten years."

Bennett was still smirking.

The Hispanic guy turned to Hotchkiss. "I don't believe half this crap."

"I do," said Hotchkiss, turning to the guy. "You haven't been here long enough to see the crap I've seen. And did you call him?" He motioned to D'Luna.

"He's who we always call."

"Not anymore," Hotchkiss told him, coming over to me. "How do you find out where this guy is?"

"If he used his own blood," I said, "I could do it with that brush."

"What if he didn't?"

"If you want it to work right, you have to use your own blood. But being that the idiot botched it right from the start, he could have used an animal's blood. There any dead animals around?"

"We'll look."

"Why?" said the guy in the suit whose name wasn't given to me.

"This is a lot of blood for someone to use. If they used fresh blood, there's a dead animal around here somewhere. If they used stored blood, then you might have to look at someone with access to a blood bank."

"You have to keep it warm and put anticoagulants in it," said Hotchkiss. "Or keep it in a sterile environment."

"And you have to use it in a few days to be viable," said the guy in the suit.

"Blood magic doesn't need to be perfect," I said. "This guy took too many shortcuts as it is."

"Are you certain it's a guy?"

"No," I said, while D'Luna said, "Yes."

Hotchkiss said, without looking at him, "You can take your cape and your Goth girl and get lost, D'Luna."

D'Luna gave me a look, an evil eye. I raised my hand, folding my middle and ring finger inward, making the sign against it. It didn't reflect it back — that's another sign — but it dissipated the energy into nothingness.

"We'll meet again," he said.

"Probably," I said, bluntly. "It's a small world."

He stalked away, his sycophant following him like a dark shadow, across the meadow. He was planning my demise, I was sure of it.

"Now, then," Hotchkiss said. "What else can you tell me?"

"Not much else, I'm afraid."

The Hispanic guy in the suit said, "Should we call a priest, too?"

Hotchkiss ignored him, turning to Bennett. "Send you the check?"

Bennett nodded. "We'll call you, kid," Hotchkiss said. He turned around and left the area, taking the Hispanic guy with him.

Bennett beckoned and we started back to his car. He smiled at me. "Good job, kid."

I glanced back at the spot where the sigil had been. The group of cops swarmed around it like bees over honey. The brush went into a plastic bag. Bits of blood and dirt were scraped up into little bags.

"What are they doing?"

"Forensics," Bennett said. "We're done here."

"But the guy who did this ..."

Bennett put an arm around my shoulders. "Leave that for the cops, Mike."

"He's done it for a reason," I persisted. "And Belial's out there somewhere."

"Leave it for the cops," he repeated, guiding me across the meadow.

"Maybe the Rosicrucians know," I murmured.

"The *who*?"

"Rosicrucians. They're magic cops." I didn't want to mention magic prison. That would be too much.

Bennett shook his head. "Magic cops, yeah, right. C'mon, let's go home."

"Hey," I said, as I got in the car, "What's this about a check?"

"They give you a consulting fee. Probably $50 an hour."

"We didn't spend an hour there."

"Plus mileage. Might get $75. I'll give you half."

I almost asked him for the whole thing, but then, I wouldn't be getting this money at all if it wasn't for him and his connections.

"Does this kind of thing happen often?"

"Magic? I don't know. I'd have to find out how often they called the other guy." He glanced at me. "You acted like you knew him."

"Met him yesterday in Salem." My phone went off. "Excuse me," I said, and flipped it open. "Hello?"

"Hi, Mikey." It was Evie. "Are you okay?"

"Yeah, I'm on my way home now."

"Oh, I was worried because you weren't home. I'm sorry if I interrupted anything."

"No, you didn't."

"Ok. How far away are you?"

I asked Bennett, "How far —"

"Fifteen minutes with this traffic."

"Fifteen —"

"I heard," she said with a light laugh. "Is that the PI?"
"Yeah. I'm on a case."
"You're a *consultant* on a case," Bennett corrected me.
I blushed. "I'm sort of on a case."
"You have to tell me all about it."
"I'm not sure you'll really want to know."

CHAPTER SEVEN

OLD HAVEN

Dom woke me up the next morning, bumping into the couch while he made his way to the computer.

"Oh, sorry, Mike."

I stretched on the couch and yawned. "It's okay. What time is it?"

"Five. I have to check and see if they gave me any work. If not, I'm going down to the police station and ask about that case you got consulted on."

"I don't think you should do that," I said.

"Why?" He turned to me while the computer booted up.

"Because one: they'll know I blabbed about it to a news reporter and I might not get called again. And two: can you imagine the wing nuts who will call in saying they've seen Belial in the flesh?" I sat up. "Not to mention how your editors might think you've gone crazy."

He sighed. Evie came into the room.

"He's right, Dom."

"I'll write a piece that they found devil worshiping implements in Slater Park," Dom said, trying to appease me. "How's that?"

"Get someone from the cops to verify," I told him. "Don't go by my word."

"I will," he said. He turned back to the computer and started typing away.

I hadn't slept well that previous night. Although Bennett said to let the cops handle it — and I thought that maybe the Rosicrucians would go chasing after the guy — I felt that it was somehow my responsibility to at least do something to help. I knew that the blood didn't belong to the person who had done it. It might very well have belonged to some animal. I didn't know if they had finally found a dead chicken or dog in the area.

"Are we going to New Haven so I can get my birth certificate?" I asked Dom.

"Oh, crap," said Dom. "I totally forgot." He stared at the screen for a minute. "Let me finish this first."

Evie put a hand on my shoulder. "He doesn't like to be interrupted when writing."

"Oh," I said.

After performing my necessary libations in the bathroom, I came out and made Evie's lunch. Dom was on a roll, though, and grumbled when he had to get up to drive Evie to work.

When he came back, he beelined right back to the computer. He sat there for almost an hour, typing constantly before he sat back. Then, he stuck his tongue out, biting it, as he re-read it. After correcting a few things, he sat back again, looking up at me.

"I've gotta make a few calls before we go," he said. "Hand me the phone?"

I grabbed the cordless phone off its charger and handed it to him. I went into the kitchen, but could still hear him talking to someone about the devil worship in Slater Park.

He made a final call to his editor. "Sure, the Wiccans might freak," Dom said. "But there's more Christians than Wiccans." He argued, cajoled, and then used logic to try and convince his editor. It didn't matter. He pressed the button to hang up and slammed the phone down on the table.

"Not good?"

"He thinks it'll piss off some religious people."

I thought about a hundred D'Lunas being pissed off. Even I wouldn't be able to stop the negative energy flowing from that kind of evil eye.

"He's got a point."

"He said something about devil worship not being a Wiccan thing. Whatever that is."

"It's not." I shook my head. "I'll tell you all about it on the drive to New Haven."

Dom hunched forward. "Do we have to go?"

"C'mon. I want to get a library card … and an ID, so I don't feel stupid when people ask me for one."

"You need something with your name and address on it. What address are you going to use?"

"The library's."

"Are you serious?"

"I can't use this one."

"Why not?"

"You live here."

"We'll be paying for you starting next week."

"I thought you were going to kick me out."

Dom gave me one of those frowning tilts of the head that said, *Are you stupid?* "No, we aren't going to kick you out. Maybe after we're married, we will."

"I hope I find something between now and then." I wondered if any of the rooms above Scott's place were available for rent.

Dom rose, stretched, and then said when he finished, "Okay, then, we'll go to New Haven."

Dom assured me that this car had gone to New Haven "plenty of times". We drove down 95, heading toward Connecticut.

"So what's a Wiccan?" he asked me.

"A Wiccan is a person who believes in nature magic. They have their own religion."

"They believe in God?"

"Gods," I said to correct him. "And Goddesses."

"Like Zeus and Apollo, and Venus and Mars?"

"Yes, exactly like that."

"Do you believe in them?"

"Yes."

"So you don't believe in God?"

"I believe in Him, too."

"But you're disobeying that First Commandment."

"I've disobeyed all of them," I said. "That doesn't make me a non-believer."

Dom drove in silence for a minute, letting that sink in. "I guess not."

"Faith is different than good works."

I didn't tell him that the way to Heaven was with both faith and good works. Let him figure that out for himself.

"You know," he said, nearly twenty minutes later, right after we got past Route 4, "I've been wondering something."

I shifted in my seat. "What's that?"

"Why did you summon that demon in the first place?"

"I wanted to punish everyone who harmed me throughout my life."

"Anyone Evie knew?"

I looked out the window for a minute. "Phil."

"Phil who?"

"Phil. My brother, Phil."

He didn't take his eyes off the road, but his body reacted. "You killed your own brother?"

"The demon did it, not me. I couldn't stop it." I didn't want to stop it. I hated him then … and even with the rosy-tinged glasses of nostalgia and time, I still hated him.

Dom slowed down behind a truck. I couldn't tell what he was thinking, but I knew that he *was* thinking. Was he going to pull over and kick me out?

"How?"

"I don't know," I said. "After Phil got out of the car, he started running across the lawn at me, and he dropped dead before I could do anything. I yelled at him to stop. The demon caused something to happen to him, I'm not sure what." I turned to look at him. "Please don't tell Evie."

"You expect me not to tell her?" He glanced for a moment at me. He was angry. He couldn't give me an intent stare that he wanted to, driving as he was. "Are you out of your mind?"

"She'll hate me."

"No kidding." He looked out at the road again. "I should just leave you out here."

"I know you don't trust me. What have I done against you? I won't hurt you, I promised her."

"You killed your own brother."

"Do you have a brother?"

"Three of them."

"Did they ever beat you up?"

"We had good-natured fights. Wrestling matches. Arguments. But God, Mike, I never thought of killing them."

"Phil was like a younger version of my father. Did Evie ever tell you about our father?"

"I've *met* your father."

"And?"

"He's a hard man to get along with."

"Spoken like a true diplomat."

"Why didn't you kill your father, then?"

"He was at the top of my list. I don't know why Belial didn't kill him. I must not have had total control. Or he didn't like the idea of fratricide. I really don't know."

I had mulled it over and over in my head. I even asked Grimalkin. He had no idea. Who knew the mind of a demon?

Dom shook his head. "I don't believe this."

"Dom. That's my past. I haven't — and I won't — do it again. I swear to God I learned my lesson — and I don't want to go back to that prison or to the Hell that awaits me."

He paused for a long time. "You're going to Hell?" he asked quietly.

"Yeah," I said, just as quietly, looking out of the windshield. "It's what happens when you traffic with demons."

"What if you go to church?"

"I believe in all the gods. But as you said, I disobeyed the First Commandment. The gates of Heaven are locked forever from me."

Dom swallowed. We drove in silence for what seemed like a long time, passing exit after exit, heading into Connecticut.

Finally, he said, "Who taught you magic?"

He was shifting subjects. Good. Maybe he accepted it. Maybe he wouldn't tell Evie.

"My Aunt Jane." I didn't mention Grimalkin.

"The one who died."

"Yes. The ones the Rosicrucians killed because she taught me magic." I tugged on the seat belt. I was getting uncomfortable, so I switched subjects. "Whatever happened to her husband?"

"He packed up and moved to Florida. Evie invited him to the wedding." We were in Connecticut in no time. He passed a few exits and a rest area. "Can anyone learn magic?" he finally asked.

"Yes," I said. "But once you learn magic, you get tempted to do more and more, until all you want is to be more and more powerful. To do that, you need entities."

"Demons?"

"Angels, demons, spirits, ifrits … you name it."

"What's ifrit?"

"Minor fire demon," I told him. "I could summon one of those with a circle and a word." At least, now I could.

"What's a circle?"

"It's a place, like a boundary. It doesn't have to be shaped like a circle, though. You use it for protection. Or to keep the power inside it until you release it. You don't always need it. For something simple, like what I did with your credit card, I didn't need a circle. I put it in the rune I drew on your card."

"That's what it's called? A rune?" He passed a big truck on the right.

"Runes, sigils, seals. That's the kind of magic I work in."

"You don't use circles?"

"Not anymore." I said. "I'm not allowed to. It's part of my release from prison."

"But what if you need it for protection?"

"Against what? I'd need a damn good reason. If the Rosicrucians found out, I'd be back in jail in minutes."

"I looked those guys up. They're associated with the Knights Templar."

I nodded. "They absorbed the Knights Templar after they were considered heretics. So were the Rosicrucians after a while. But they're now God's cops and jailers."

"Okay, stupid question: Why can't you use fireballs?"

"I can."

He turned to me for a half-second, taking his eyes off the road. "No way."

"Yes, way. But first, it takes an awful lot of power to break reality like that. You see, people have their own sense of reality. It permeates everything. This is a car. It rides on four wheels. It doesn't fly."

"Unless you hit a bump a certain way."

"Granted. But in general, it doesn't fly. That's reality. You know it, and I know it. I could overpower your will — your belief — that this car can fly. I could use that firm, unequivocal belief, and attach it to my own will and make this car fly. But everyone who sees it, I have to bend their reality to agree with my — now our — reality. I have to use will to either force them to believe that this car is flying, which takes a lot of power and will on my part. Or I can trick them, like a stage magician does."

"Can you do that kind of stuff? Saw ladies in half?"

"Oh, please."

"No?"

"No."

He took the next exit to New Haven's government offices. He drove around the city hall, looking for a parking spot. "Do you know any tricks to find a parking spot?"

I muttered the spell under my breath as he went around a second time. I aimed with my index finger and, a few feet ahead of us, someone pulled out of a spot. It was a block away from the city hall, which wasn't that bad.

"Isn't that a coincidence," Dom said, as he pulled into the spot. I just smiled.

Dom put money in the meter — just in case, although it had half an hour left on it — and we walked to the city hall.

"I see you've been this way before," I said.

"Evie got her wallet stolen a few years' back when I was first dating her."

"How long have you guys been going out?"

"You had disappeared for about two years when we met, so almost three years now?"

"How did you meet?"

He laughed. "I'll tell you all about it on the way home."

We went up the stairs to the City Hall building, and I followed Dom to the clerk's office. It was just after 11, but there was no one at the counter. A woman got up from one of the desks beyond it, a very large woman with a shock of white hair and thick horn-rimmed glasses. She seemed to waddle over to us. "Can I help you?"

"I need my birth certificate," I said.

"Do you have anything with your name and address on it?"

"Dammit. Look, I just got out of prison. I don't have anything except my release papers."

"Do you have them?"

"I can get them. Do you have a piece of paper and a black marker?"

She raised an eyebrow at me. "Yes," she said, and got both.

Dom watched as I took them both out of the office. I heard him say, "He wasn't in jail for stealing."

I found a small table hidden away in a corner. The least exposure, the better. With the marker, I drew a summoning circle on the paper. God, I hoped that Ritter wouldn't leap out of an office and grab me. My command was for the release papers, which were located on the end table in Evie's apartment, folded up. I stood above the sheet of paper, my hands above the circle, and closed my eyes.

"*Voluntati meae,*" I began in Latin. "*Hæc mando liber apparere hic locus de oculo mentis meae.*" By my will, I command the paper to appear from the place of my mind's eye.

It was a simple spell, since I could picture exactly where the items were. I'd practiced this kind of spell in prison. One of the old witches had taught me simple teleportation of objects.

The papers appeared, first translucent, reflecting the area they were located. I could see in the reflection of the cordless phone jack that was right next to it. I pulled with my will, and the papers solidified, fully appearing within the center of that circle.

I plucked my papers from the circle seconds before the paper on which the circle was drawn caught fire, and I batted it out before it would set off sprinklers. Dom stepped outside. "I thought I smelled something burning."

I slid the burnt paper in the trash. "Nope, all set."

The summoning circle had consumed itself, so the only thing left was the burnt paper, without any evidence of what it had been used for.

I walked into the clerk's office, and held the papers up. "Here they are!" I unfolded them, glanced at them.

Yeah, they were my release papers all right — including the voucher for the taxi driver. I slipped that out. Written in calligraphy, they looked like they could be used as a certificate, but they had the seal of the prison, the seal of the Knights Templar, and a bunch of official-looking and sounding terms that said, basically, I was a free man with "certain provisions discussed prior to release".

The woman wrinkled up her nose and took my papers. She must have tried to read the archaic and fancy language because her eyes squinted. She put the papers down and looked at Dom.

"Do you attest he is who he says he is?"

"I do."

"Who are you?"

"Soon-to-be brother-in-law."

"No one in the family is here?" she asked me.

I leaned forward. "He's practically family." I stared deep in her eyes and pushed forward, just a little bit, with my will. "Believe me," I commanded.

She didn't blink. She didn't move an inch. "You believe us and you will get the birth certificate, and you will not charge us anything for it. Say it."

"I will believe you and get your birth certificate and not charge you."

I snapped my fingers. She blinked, looked at me. She passed the papers back to me. "What's your birthday?"

"April 18, 1982."

"I'll be right back."

Dom came over to me when she left, "Mike, did you hypnotize her?"

"Yep." I brushed my fingernails against my chest and blew on them. "New trick, didn't know if it would work out here."

The clerk came back with a heavy black book. "April-July 1982" was emblazoned on the front. She opened the book, and it was indexed by date. Then, it was indexed by child's last name. She found me smack dab in the middle.

After making a copy of the certificate, she stamped it, signed it, and then handed it to me. "Thank you," I said.

"You're welcome. Have a good day."

I folded the birth certificate into thirds, then in half, and tucked it in my jeans. "There. Now all I need is something sent to the library and I'll be all set."

"You really weren't going to send it to the library?"

"Why not?"

"Won't they just throw it out?"

"Not if I ask them nicely."

"You mean hypnotize them."

"I wouldn't do such a thing! I have a good relationship there."

When we got back to the car. I asked Dom, "You wouldn't be able to take me to my family, would you?"

"I thought you wanted to leave your parents out of it."

"I mean, since we're here."

Dom shrugged.

"My father's still working, right?"

"He's doing account sales at some insurance company. He lost his job after you disappeared, and Evie almost didn't go to Brown. She had to take out some serious debt."

I frowned. "And mom?"

"She's working at Yale New Haven Hospital in the neonatal unit."

"She's a nurse?"

My mother was not nursing material. I remember when I used to get colds or headaches, she'd send me to school anyway. And if I came home sick, she'd send me to my bed with adult-grade cough syrup and tell me to sleep it off.

"No, she's a clerk. Works something like 30 hours a week."

"Do they live in the same old house?"

"They sold it a couple of years ago. They live in a condo."

"Condo?"

"Condominium. It's like you own your own apartment. They can be fancy."

"Is theirs fancy?"

"No, but they have a nice view of trees out back."

They used to own their own house on the western side of town, a house with a yard and a garage, two floors and a finished basement. Their condo wasn't really in town, but out in the suburbs. It was nothing really to write home about, as it looked to me like all the other buildings around it. It had a neat, well-kept lawn, no decorations, no flower pots, and no flowers under the front bay window. A concrete driveway ran up a short hill to a garage. Its tiny front door held no decorations for the season.

Dom parked in front of the building. An unfamiliar car sat parked in the driveway. "That's mom's car," said Dom, putting the car into park.

"No," I said.

"No, what?"

"No, I don't want to get out."

"I thought you —"

"No," I said. "No, just get out of here."

He shrugged, put the car back into drive, and we drove to the end of the street. It was a round dead-end area, with more of those cookie-cutter houses. I felt sick to my stomach.

"I'm not ready," I told him.

"It's cool," said Dom. "Maybe by the time the wedding comes."

I changed the subject without a clutch. "So you didn't tell me how you guys met."

He smiled as we pulled out of the gated community, and I felt a little better.

"How we met …" Dom said wistfully. We headed through the side streets of suburbia toward the highway. "We both were attending Brown. I was a freshman. She was a sophomore."

"I thought you were older than her."

"I am," he replied. "Two years older. I had to help my dad with the store. You know, family is a free labor source."

"Yeah, I get that. So here you are in Brown …"

"Yeah. We both had an astronomy class. We both went to the observatory to look at some moon thing. There's this tiny platform at the bottom of the telescope and only two people can stay on it at one time. There was a set of six metal steps leading down onto a concrete floor. We were both standing on the platform."

"So you asked her out?"

"I wanted to. I kept looking at her out of the corner of my eye. I didn't pay attention, but I pretended to, making some stupid notes on the notebook. Then my time was up and I turned around. I bumped into her. I stepped back, tripped, and fell right down those stairs right on my face."

"Oh, my God — no way!"

He laughed. "Yeah. There I was, in front of the whole class, and here she comes, running down the stairs with a tissue. She put it on my split lip and held it there. It was the most beautiful thing she did."

"You asked her out then?"

"No, the next class. I still remember — I said, 'I know I'm a klutz, but will you come to dinner with me as long as I don't carry anything?'"

"And she said yes?"

He chuckled. "Of course, she said yes."

"So where was your first date?"

"Kabob and Curry on Thayer. Then we went to Ben & Jerry's around the corner." He was silent for a bit. "I heard all about how *way* more dysfunctional your family is than mine."

"What about your family?"

He mused for a moment as he changed lanes. "Dad owned a drug store until the big chains built down the street. He's retired now."

"And mom?"

"She died a couple of years ago. I probably wouldn't have survived if Evie hadn't been there."

"You and your mom were close?"

Dom shrugged. "Italian mothers can be just as demanding as Italian fathers. She wanted me to go to school. I didn't think I had the grades to get into Brown, but I did."

"So now you're a reporter."

"Stringer." He glanced at me. "Hey, want to take me to the place that you went to yesterday? With that demon thing?"

Was Fate working her wicked will? I had wanted to go back there myself.

"Sure," I said, hoping I sounded nonchalant.

CHAPTER EIGHT

NEW INFORMATION

WE GOT TO THE PARK IN JUST UNDER TWO HOURS. Although I was hungry, because my stomach growled, I instead directed Dom past the little outdoor restaurant that wasn't open. We parked in a dirt parking lot which faced the field, a group of trees stood on either side of it. I told Dom to wait in the car. He pouted, but he sat there anyway.

They hadn't covered the area up, but had taken the tape down. And standing in the clearing was Ritter, wearing his gray felt fedora and black suit.

"You're just the man I was hoping to run into," I said.

He crossed his arms and glared at me. "Do you surrender?"

"For what?"

"Summoning this demon."

I rolled my eyes so hard I felt it. "C'mon. I didn't summon this demon."

Ritter thrust his hands in his pockets. If he didn't truly believe me, he would have rushed me like he did when he took me down the first time we had met. "Prove it."

"I was sleeping."

"Did you dream?"

"I don't remember." Ritter started to advance. "Wait," I told him, putting my hands up. "Will you please listen to me? We have to find the guy who did this."

"Why?"

"He's possessed and he'll be dead. Where's your Pathfinder?"

Pathfinders and Knights worked with other members of a Hunting Team to find those people who had summoned demons or committed other nefarious magical workings. The Pathfinder was the one who could track and find the demon and the person who summoned it.

Ritter seemed to rock a little. "I don't need a Pathfinder for what I need."

"Tracking me?"

"Waiting for you to screw up, Grimaulkin. And you *will* screw up. What did you return to the scene of the crime for?"

"Oh, for God's sake," I said, throwing my hands up in the air. "Look, no matter what I do, I'll always be the prisoner in 104 to you. But I'm not the same angry kid who went into prison. I'm a different man, now. So will you *please* let me try and help someone who obviously screwed up?"

Ritter walked over toward me, and stood on opposite side of the sigil. "If you join forces with this person, I will put you down like a rabid dog."

"I'd want you to, Ritter."

He jerked back as if I'd hit him in the face. I don't think he expected that. Hell, I hadn't expected it. He recovered pretty quickly, made a *humpf* sound, and walked past me to the field. He went to a car that was parked a little bit beyond where Dom sat waiting.

With Ritter gone, I could concentrate now. I turned back to the spot with the sigil. There was one spell that I knew that might be able to help me find the guy. It wasn't a Pathfinder's spell — those were proprietary and Grimalkin didn't know those — but I knew one that was close to it.

I crouched and placed my right hand on my solar plexus. My left hand dug into the dirt where the sigil had been. My non-dominant hand, my left, was receptive. I breathed deeply, putting myself into a light trance. I uttered the spell, in Enochian, "Take me back, back to the time before, of he who had this object." Of course, Enochian sounds much cooler.

I closed my eyes and, in my mind's eye, I could see the cops walking around the place, someone brushing the dirt over the blood. I kept saying, "Back" to force the everything to move backwards. Cops moved backward, like a rewinding tape; the dirt was brushed away.

Nothing else happened for a long while. Day turned to night, then a flash of red light with red smoke appeared.

"Back," I said, and the flash disappeared.

Next came a man's face, set deep in concentration, painting on the ground, steadying himself with his left hand pressing into the grass. A bowl is set to the side, as he dips the brush and paints, over and over.

He is pale-skinned, with very short black hair. He's far older than me, maybe in his early 30's, with stubble for a beard — he hasn't shaved in a few days. He has brown eyes and a square jaw with a hint of a jowl. His build seems a little porky, but not severely. He lifts his hand quickly from the side of the circle, which means to me he has bad balance.

I pulled my hand away from the dirt, saving the man's face in my mind. I thanked the Powers That Be for their guidance, and sat back.

"I know what you look like."

⊛   ⊛   ⊛

Not sure what to do with this new information, I debated with myself whether to go to the police. Just because I had his face in mind didn't mean I knew who he was.

"Did you get his name?" asked Dom, when I got back to the car and told him what I knew.

I frowned and said, "C'mon. That would be too easy." I stared at the group of trees. My hunger was gone, transformed into a sick pit in the middle of my stomach. "Belial came too fast for him to do anything. He couldn't have stopped him if he tried."

"So what do we do now?"

"I don't know, that's the problem. Do I go to the cops? Will they believe me?"

"What about the PI?"

"That sounds like a good idea," I said. "Maybe he can at least talk to them for me."

"Let's get something to eat, first. I'm starving."

"You got any money?"

Dom grinned. "I don't give Evie *everything*, you know."

He stopped at a bank, took out some money from the ATM, and we went around the corner from the bank to a corner diner.

We had wieners. Wieners are a Rhode Island thing. Known in Rhode Island as New York System Wieners, I don't think they're really sold in New York. They consist of a hot dog, but not just any hot dog — only small crunchy ones with the ends of the dogs cut off (if done right). Mustard, a meat sauce, chopped onions, and celery salt top the hot dog. I ordered three, thinking they were like chili dogs (which I'm ambivalent about), but for some reason they were very filling, and two would have been perfect. As it was, I felt too full to finish off the fries, but Dom did.

After lunch, I had Dom drive me to Bennett's office; I told him I'd walk home. Dom left, and I went upstairs to see Bennett. I knocked on his door and then I peered through the frosted glass window on the side of the door.

Nothing moved inside. I put my ear to the door, and didn't hear the TV or anything.

"Crap," I muttered, and went back downstairs. I had left my phone at the house because I was with Dom, so I didn't have a way to call him. I didn't have his number, even if I did have my phone.

I walked back home, but I got sick half way there and threw up in the gutter.

I was so sick that I passed out on the couch. No more wieners for me. Ever.

I woke up in the middle of the night and forced myself to have peanut butter on toast with some water. I would have liked ginger ale, but it was far too late at night to go out and get some.

The next morning, I felt much better. Dom got up, checked his computer, and said, "I have to go to the Y. Want to come?"

"I think so," I said. "Do you have an extra pair of swimming trunks?"

Dom nodded and got a pair of shorts for me. I had another toast and peanut butter with tea.

Dom picked me up after dropping off Evie at school. We drove down to the Y, had to park in the parking garage and walk up the hill.

I went to the weight room and worked out, but not as hard as I usually did. My stomach was still kind of flippy. I was the only person in the gym for a while, but then a heavy-set guy came in. He took a spot on the treadmill, but only walked the entire time I was there. He listened to a tiny Walkman or something like one attached to his waist, with wires leading up to his ears. He walked constantly, building up a sweat.

I did weights, sit-ups, crunches, lifts, push-ups — all the things I had done in prison, in the same order, with the same method. Muscle memory carried me through and, as I mindlessly did the work out, I filled out the picture of the man I saw in my head at the park.

He was older than me. He wore a button-down shirt, which meant to me, at least, that he was either a businessman or a nerd. Not a nerd, I decided. He didn't have pens in the pocket of his shirt. I didn't see below his waist, but guessed he had worn khakis with loafers.

I finished my workout and, covered in sweat and feeling a thousand times better, I pulled out the swimming trunks, went to the locker room and changed. After I'd finished a few laps in the pool, I got out, dried off, and went back to the locker room to get dressed.

I found Dom in the office with the woman we had seen the first day we were there.

"Hello," I said to both of them. "Dom, I'm going to the library."

"Okay."

"When do you want me to come back?"

He glanced at the computer, and then at the woman. "About an hour?"

"I'll be back then." I noted that my phone had a clock on it; it was 11:30.

✦ ✦ ✦

Scott's store should be open, I thought, changing my mind from the library. I left the Y and went to downtown to the store.

He came out from the back room as I entered. "Hey," he said, giving me a smile.

"Hey," I said, smiling also. "How's business?"

"Good. I have a card reading at twelve, so I'll have to kick you out soon."

"That's all right. Do you have any sea salt?"

He pointed to the herb wall. "Third shelf from the bottom."

I saw the jar full of white crystals. I went over and picked it up. "Can I pay you later?"

"When is 'later'?"

"When Bennett gets money from the Pawtucket Police."

He snorted. "That could be months." He took out a notebook from under the counter, wrote something out. "Here, sign this."

At the top of the page was written in perfect cursive letters, "I promise to pay the below total to Scott Angrier or the White Raven." I signed on the line he had drawn. He signed below it,

"You know," I said. "You can magically go after me with that."

"It's to go after you legally if I have to."

"Once Bennett gives me the money, I'll bring it to you."

He shrugged.

"Speaking of Bennett, do you have his number?"

"I have the number to his office, but not his new cell phone number. Why?"

"I want to get a hold of him. We're sort of working on a case together."

"Did he ever call you on your phone? You can see who called you."

"Yeah. Yeah, he did." I took out my phone and handed it to Scott.

He showed me how to scroll down to the right menu, select "Calls" and there was a list of people who had called me. Dom was first — he had called me yesterday. I scrolled through and found a number I didn't know. I memorized it and called it (not realizing I could just press the green button on the phone to call).

"Hello?"

"Frank?"

"Who's this?"

"It's Mike."

"How did you get this number?"

"The magic of technology," I said. "Amazing, huh? Listen, are you around? I need to talk to you."

"I'm kind of busy right now." In the background, I heard what sounded like an auctioneer over a loudspeaker, announcing numbers.

"Okay. When you're done?"

"It won't be until late."

"You know where I live. Call me before you come down and I'll wait for you outside."

"Yeah, okay." He hung up before I could say good-bye. I looked at the phone. "Well, that was short."

"He's at the track," said Scott. "Or the casino."

"He has a gambling problem?"

"I wouldn't call it a problem. If he has any extra money, he goes and spends it at the track. He doesn't owe bookies or anything."

"Then I guess that's not a problem." I put the phone away. "So." I leaned on the counter. "When I get paid, how about we go out to dinner sometime."

He blushed as he weighed out the salt. "How much?"

"Six ounces."

He used the metal scoop inside the jar and weighed out six ounces of salt. "What're you going to do with this?"

"You didn't answer my question."

"I didn't think you asked one."

"I think I was asking you on a date."

And this time, a fire truck with sirens blaring went by. We stopped what we were doing as it stopped just outside. "Must be something at the DMV," he said.

"The DMV?"

"Yeah, it's that big red building over there." He motioned out the front window. He handed me the packet of salt in a small plastic bag, sealed at the top.

"What's a DMV?"

He looked at me quizzically. "Department of Motor Vehicles? Where you go and get your driver's license."

"Oh! I, um, I don't drive."

"Where are you from, originally?"

"New Haven, Connecticut. I've been, um, out of the country for a few years." Which was sort of true, since the William F. Blackstone prison didn't allow the inmates to contact the outside world, and all of the books in their library were at least 20 years old.

"They don't have DMV's where you went?"

"Nope."

"Where did you go?"

"Greece."

"Whereabouts?"

"Troy."

He smiled. "Troy isn't in Greece."

I know I blushed, because I felt my face get hot. I looked away from him.

"Why won't you tell me the truth?"

"Because you wouldn't want to go out with me."

"And what makes you think I would go out with you if you lied?"

I sighed; he had me there. I looked at him again. He didn't look angry. In fact, he seemed more amused instead.

"I've been in prison for the last five years."

"Prison?" He stepped away from the counter. "For what?"

"Summoning a demon."

"Wait ... what?"

"Haven't you heard of the Rosicrucians?"

He shook his head.

"They're the magic cops."

"Seriously?" He blinked. "There's magic cops?"

I nodded. "They probably haven't come here because you're not doing bad things or selling spells to do bad things."

Scott leaned back against the wall. "You can go to prison for summoning a demon?"

"If they catch you. They didn't catch me the first time."

"How many times did you summon demons?"

"Twice. Once when I was 11, and the second time when I was 12, just turning 13."

"You really summoned demons."

"Yes."

He looked at me, a little wide-eyed. "I knew you had a dark aura, but I didn't suspect that." He glanced at the back room for a minute. "However, that explains why you were described as having a bad past. I thought it was that you were abused or something."

"You did a reading about me?"

He blushed again. "Well, yeah."

"What else did it say?"

"I'd rather not say."

I really wanted to know, and probably would have pressed him, but the door opened, and a woman entered the store. She wore a dress and heels, looked like she probably worked in an office. "Hi," she said. "I know I'm early."

"It's okay," Scott said to her. "I'll just need a few minutes to get things ready." He looked pointedly at me. "Come back later?"

"I'll try," I said. "If not, I'll be here tomorrow."

"That's good," he said. He smiled at me, and went into the back room.

I pocketed the salt packet and left. As I walked up the hill to the library, I wondered. *Did he say yes to the date?*

CHAPTER NINE

MEETING NEW PEOPLE

I WENT TO THE LIBRARY, noting its address as I entered. Jessica was at the front desk and smiled at me when I came in.

"Hi," she said.

"Hi," I replied. "I think I'm ready for that library card. Can you accept a birth certificate as proof?"

"Yes, I think so." She pulled out a form from a drawer and handed it to me. "Just fill this out."

Of course, they asked for an address. I filled in the library's address anyway, hoping they wouldn't notice. When I finished, she entered it into the computer without batting an eye. She pulled out a plastic card, scanned its bar number, did a little more typing, and then handed me the card. I realized I was going to need a wallet pretty soon.

I smiled at her. "Thank you, hon."

She blushed a deep shade of red. I chuckled and headed to the rear stacks. I picked out a cookbook for "modern busy cooks", a biography of Marlon Brando, *Bag of Bones* by Stephen King, and *The Tipping Point* by Malcolm Gladwell. I was so used to reading eclectically, because of the small selection of books in the prison, that I had no idea what I liked anymore. There were no books on magic, or even spirituality, in the prison. There were no fiction books with magic in them — not even *The Lord of the Rings* series.

Taking my treasures with me, I walked across the street to the Y. Dom wasn't done when I arrived. In fact, he didn't get done until almost two o'clock. He didn't have time to go pick up Evie from school, so he called her to tell her he was going to be late. She told him that it was okay, she would hitch a ride home from someone.

When Dom finally finished, we returned to the apartment. We were starving, so we tore through the place, putting together some macaroni and cheese, finally eating at around three.

I got a phone call while I had a mouthful of macaroni and cheese.

"Hey," said Frank. "I'll be there in half an hour."

"Okay," I said, trying not to stuff my face with more macaroni at that moment. I finished my plate, and walked downstairs to wait.

The landlady looked out the window at me. I smiled and waved. I received a disgusted look back. I went to the front of the house and waited outside of the wire fence. A light blue car pulled up soon after I leaned back against the fence.

Evie stepped out of the car's passenger side. "Oh, hi, Mikey."

"Hi," I said, and gave her a kiss.

"Is that your fiancé?" came a voice from inside the car. I bent down to look. A woman sat in the driver's seat. She wore a light blue shirt, with raven hair, and deep brown eyes. Her skin was a shade darker than mine.

Evie laughed. "No, it's my brother. Mikey, this is Patricia."

"Hi," I said with a wave.

"Hi," she said with a smile and maybe she was blushing.

"She's in the classroom down the hall from me," said Evie. "We go to lunch together."

I smiled. She was looking at me the way women looked at guys they were interested in. Not quite hungry, but not quite demure. More like a shy checking-out. I'm sure Evie was going to get asked tomorrow whether I was available or not.

I stood up straight as Evie said, "What are you doing out here?"

"Waiting for someone."

"Ah." She bent down to look in the window. "Thanks again, Patricia. I'll see you tomorrow."

"Anytime, Evie. Nice to meet you!" she called to me, and pulled out into the street.

I sighed. "You're going to have to break her heart."

"What do you mean?" Evie tilted her head, curious.

"She's going to ask you about me and you're going to have to tell her I don't bat for that team."

She laughed, and then punched my arm. "She married, silly." She walked to the house.

Bennett was on time, pulling into a parking spot in front of the house next door. He got out, not bothering to lock the door. "Hey," he said. He smelled like booze and cigarettes.

"Hey. I went back to the place you brought me to yesterday."

"And?"

"I know what the guy looks like."

"Think you can describe him to a sketch artist?"

"Well, do you think they'd believe me?"

"How did you find out?"

"I touched the ground."

"You can do that?"

"Only if I have to."

"Would you stake your life on it?"

I thought about it. "My ability or what I saw?"

"Both. Because if we go to the police with this, they'll put out an APB to every corner of the state, hold a press conference, and people will be looking for this guy everywhere. You'll have to pick out this guy in a line-up. If you're one bit wrong, not only will you lose any credibility with the police, but you'll have half the state angry at you."

"Only half?"

"The other half won't care."

My joke wasn't serious, and it covered up my thinking. "Maybe I shouldn't. It could be someone who stepped near there. This guy was older than me, a businessman, I think." As I tried to recreate him in my mind, the images remained foggy. His hands, for one. Did he have gloves? It had been such a flash, I wasn't sure anymore. That's one sign of a bad feeling: second guessing.

"Describe him to me."

I did the best I could: his chiseled face, brown eyes and hair, body bent over the spot I had touched, painstakingly painting the sigil in the dirt. His shirt was clear to me, an off-white, almost grey, button-down shirt with a breast pocket. "It was rolled up to his elbows."

Bennett nodded. "Could be anybody. Do you think you could pick him out of a picture book or a lineup?"

I shook my head. If given a set of faces to look at, I knew they'd all blur and look the same after a while.

"At least you're honest, Mike," Bennett said. He paused, then offhandedly mentioned, "You know some lady is watching us through the window over there."

"That's our nosy landlady."

"Ah." He turned and, I suspected, looked directly at her. He looked back at me. "She's gone now."

"Did you win anything at the casino?"

"I never do."

"Then why play?"

He shrugged. "Gives me something to do."

I heard the side door slam close. Evie and Dom walked out hand-in-hand.

Dom said, "We're going on our weekly visit to my dad's. Want to come?"

Evie looked up at Bennett, who nodded to her. I looked between the two and realized introductions were in order.

"Oh, Evie, Dom? This is Frank Bennett, the PI I told you about."

Dom and Evie shook hands with him.

"I'm sorry, I have to be going anyway," said Bennett. "A pleasure." He walked back to his car.

"Sure," I said to Dom and Evie. "I'll go."

We drove to a high-rise apartment complex that sat on the banks of a river in a town called Cumberland. It was an idyllic place, except for the high-rise. We parked near an area that had benches and small square concrete tables. They overlooked the river and some woods to one side of the big building.

After unfolding myself from the back seat of the car, we walked to the main entrance with a foyer. Mounted on the wall was a list of people with their last names on a board. Below the list was a small number pad with a speaker beside it.

Dom entered a code on the number pad and then pressed the button next to the speaker. "Dad, it's me."

I heard a buzz, and the glass door in front of us unlocked. Dom held the door for Evie and me to enter. We went past two old ladies, past more old people, and it hit me that this was housing for the elderly.

"How old is your father, anyway?" I asked.

"Seventy," Dom said quietly. He seemed embarrassed. I didn't press him.

After getting off from an elevator on the sixth floor, we turned left down a corridor.

It smelled like old people here, I don't know how to describe it — a combination of mold and decay with a hospital smell overlaying it all. We arrived at a white door with the number 612 painted on it in gold. Dom pounded on it, loud enough to echo through the hallway.

The man who opened the door was angry. At least he didn't look happy at seeing us.

He glowered at Dom. "What do you want?"

"To say 'Hi', Dad."

He grumbled and stepped away from the door. I could hear the TV in the other room.

"Who is it?" yelled a woman's voice as we stepped inside.

"Dominic," said the father.

"Who?"

"DOMINIC."

Dom entered the room while Evie and I stayed in the kitchen area.

"Hi, Maggie," he said.

"Hi, Dominic! Where's your little lady?"

Dom stretched his hand out, and Evie stepped forward.

"Oh, hi, Evelyn."

I snickered. Only mom called her Evelyn. Evie didn't see me do it, though.

Evie glanced at me. "I brought my brother." She had to yell it to Maggie.

Evie beckoned me, and I stood beside her.

"Hi," I said in a loud voice.

"Hello."

Both his father and the woman studied me. While his father was a short, dumpy guy with a gut that hung over his belt, the woman was waif-like thin, with thin bones and long arms. Her thinning hair was tied back in a bun. She wore thick bottle-bottom glasses and a housecoat that just barely covered her knobby knees.

I must have passed the father's test, because he turned to Dom. "Get a job yet?"

"Dad," he said with a sigh, "I have a job."

"Does it have health insurance? Time off? A steady income?" I thought his father was going to keep on going. But he ended his tirade with, "Then it's not a job."

"It's hard to get in the journalism business, dad."

Maggie started to rise. It took her a long time for her to get to her feet, and I wondered if I should go help her. But she stood with the help of a cane.

"Let's let the boys catch up," she said, putting her hand on Evie's arm and leaned on her as they went into the kitchen.

Dom's father immediately turned down the TV. "Well, siddown."

I sat next to Dom on the couch.

The father sat in one of those huge reclining chairs, one with enough padding to hide a body in.

"What's your name?"

"Mike."

"What do you do for work?"

"I'm helping out a private investigator."

He perked up. "With what?"

I glanced at Dom. Dom shook his head just a little bit.

"Stakeouts," I said. "Nothing important."

"See? I sent you to school, and for what, Dominic?"

Dom sat there.

"You can get a job in an office somewhere, can't you? You can use computers."

"Dad, I went to school for *journalism*."

"Where's the money in that?" The father looked at me. "Did you go to school?"

"No," I said.

The father turned to Dom. "Now why can't you get a good job like Mike, here."

I almost burst out laughing. Instead, I tried to pull Dom out from under the bus. "I'm more or less on call. It's not really that great of a job."

Now Dom's father gave me a disgusted look. "You don't have a steady job, either?"

"I just got here," I said. If Dom wasn't going to give it back to him, then I was going to.

He turned away. "What is it with kids these days? What happened to getting real jobs?"

"It's hard to break into journalism," said Dom again. "I have to start somewhere, and being a stringer is a good starting point."

"You think you're going to work for the *Pawtucket Times* after all this time?"

"I hope so," Dom said.

"Why not work for the *Journal*?"

"I didn't get into their intern program. I got into the *Times'* program, and they hired me as a stringer. Eventually I'll get my own byline."

"And then it'll be a full-time job?"

"Possibly."

Meanwhile I could hear yelling from the kitchen. It was a typical conversation, being held at high volume. But it distracted me, because I honestly didn't like this dressing down that poor Dom was getting from his father. I didn't think it fair.

Then they started talking about politics and I tuned them out. I watched the TV, not paying attention to it, thinking about what the guy with Belial was doing — or was going to do. Had he done something already?

When I summoned Belial, I let the spirit go. I knew that it wouldn't last very long in the world without a vessel. However, if it possessed a person or living creature, it could last days. A spirit would last only a night — maybe 24 hours, tops.

The spirit, the demon without a vessel, used magic to make things happen. So could a possessed person, as the demon could use that person's will to augment the magic and force things to happen. However, people often had their own roadblocks to magic, and the demon would have to somehow force the person to give up their will to make things happen. It wasn't pretty.

I could only imagine the guy, the businessman in the button-down shirt, had gotten himself in way over his head. I wanted to save him, to have him "see the light" as it were, but I knew Belial wouldn't let the guy go without a fight.

Dom got up from the couch. I suspected that it was time to go, so I got up, too.

"We'll see you next week," Dom said to his father.

"Yeah," said his father, looking at the TV.

Dom claimed Evie from the yelling Maggie, who gave me a peck on the cheek in farewell. We walked out into the relative quiet of the hallway.

Evie put her hand to her forehead. "I need an aspirin."

"I can cure that," I said.

"No, it's okay," Dom said. "We have a bottle in the car just for this contingency."

The next morning, Dom was already up, showered and dressed. "They got me working the police blotter."

"What's that mean?"

"I have to go report on silly things the police did overnight: fires, rescues, domestic violence."

"Fun," I stated sarcastically.

Evie was also dressed, but yawning. "Stop at Dunkin'," she said. "I need a coffee."

"It's almost payday!" said Dom happily. "We can do that. You need a ride anywhere, Mike? Because I'll have the car all day."

"I'll walk to downtown."

Fifteen minutes later, the apartment was empty, except for me and Rufus. I took Rufus out for his walk — I had inherited that duty, it seemed — and fed him breakfast as I took the last of the bread to make toast.

Downtown was a half-hour's walk. I had seen buses go by, but wasn't sure about their schedule. I had been taught from an early age not to go on buses alone: they were full of the dregs of society and I could get attacked there. I could get attacked while walking, too. But in a bus, it was an enclosed space with nowhere to go. I knew this from experience.

Two days before I was arrested, I was beaten up so severely on my school bus that the monitor had to walk me to my door (to the angry yelling of the bus driver to just leave me at the corner). My mother wasn't home, but the monitor left me on the stoop, battered and bleeding, and with a concussion.

I fleetingly thought I should have killed that bus driver. I forced myself to let the thought go. I can't have thoughts like that anymore. I can't.

Anyway, for that reason, going on a bus on my own wasn't my most favorite thing in the world. So around 9:30, I left the house and walked to downtown Pawtucket.

By the time I was halfway there, the sky began spitting rain. I didn't have a jacket or an umbrella; I should have checked the forecast.

By the time I got to the Y, I was soaked through to the bone. I was glad I'd left a clean set of clothes in the locker. I checked my locker. I had sealed it with a magic spell, not a combination lock, as I didn't have any of those at hand. I spelled the locker open.

I stripped down. As I did, a man came into the locker room. He was about my height, dark-skinned, older than me by a good ten years, with a beard and tattoos. I noticed one of his tattoos was a pentacle being carried on a string by a flying bird of paradise. Even on his black skin, the colors were striking.

He caught me staring. He gave me a look, and I smiled.

"Nice tattoo."

He looked down at his left pec, where the tattoo was. "Thanks," he said though he sounded embarrassed, like Bennett had when I asked him about the casino.

I held out my hand. "I'm Mike."

"Max." He shook my hand. He was strong. "You're new here."

"Yep. Just joined up last week."

"Cool."

He set down his bag, started pulling out his clothes, and got undressed right in front of me. I will admit, I was happy I still had my jeans on, because if I'd been wearing sweats and he was doing that in front of me … Yeah, something would be noticeable.

"See you out there," he said. He left his bag there, but put his wallet and keys in a locker.

I debated whether a cold shower was in order before I went out to the gym. However, the good thing about being a wizard, especially if you're a wizard who did a lot of meditation and body regulation during the past five years, is that you can control your body's reactions. Most of the time.

Emotions caused the body to react. I had to possess a cold, emotional detachment from that hunk of beefcake that was in the gym waiting for me. I closed my eyes, took a few deep breaths, and finally felt calm enough to go out there.

I went to the weight room. He was there, running on a treadmill. I started with weights. I concentrated on the reps. If I let my mind wander, it would go to places that it shouldn't go. I made myself present in the moment, feeling my body resist the weights, the pull of gravity, counting the reps instead of sensing when the time would be over for them, just as I had done during this workout every day for a good four years.

I switched it up, working on the glutes, then the abs. I was so involved with my workout that I didn't notice him leave. Part of me was sad when I finally noticed that he left; another part of me wanted to show off for him.

I finished my workout with a run on the treadmill, the same one he had run on. I strained to try and feel his essence, but I couldn't run and work my will at the same time.

It didn't matter, I supposed. He wasn't really my type.

I walked back to the locker room, and saw Max in the hallway, his gym bag slung over his shoulder, heading out. "Hey, man," he said.

"Hey," I replied.

He asked me, "Where'd you learn how to lift like that?"

"Greece."

"What do you bench?"

"350."

Max whistled. "Damn. I can't press more than 300."

I looked him over. He was a little bigger than me, but not taller. "You weigh, what, 150?"

"153."

"You doing this for weight or strength?"

"Weight, actually."

"Then what you're lifting is fine. I'm doing it for strength." I had to act the part if I looked it.

He nodded. "Okay, then. You gotta teach me some of those lifts."

"I don't know the names of them. I learned them by watching someone else."

"Gotcha. I'll see you later."

"Later," I said, and watched his butt in his tight jeans as he walked out. I sighed, and went to the locker room to go to the pool.

I walked quickly in the rain down to The White Raven, carrying my backpack with my wet clothes in one hand. Scott was at the front when I walked in, frowning.

"Everything all right?" I asked.

"Not going to be very many people coming in today," he said, motioning to the windows.

"Time to take inventory."

"Did that a couple of weeks ago."

"Did you have lunch?" At the thought, my stomach growled, but not loud enough for him to hear, thank goodness.

"No," he said.

"You buy, I'll fly," I said. "Chinese?" I gestured out the windows, meaning to point toward the China Inn, located beyond at the end of the street. "I promise I'll get the cheapest thing on the menu."

Scott rummaged around under the counter and came up with their menu. "Get what you want," he said. "I'm putting this on your tab."

"Fine with me," I said, and picked out the cheapest thing on the menu: Egg Foo Yung.

"I'll take an L 12," he said, which was beef with broccoli. He gave me the money and I went back out into the rain.

The restaurant was busy, though it really didn't take long for our order to be ready. At least it didn't seem that way, because I was playing with my phone, trying to figure it out. I had gotten to the phone's menu and had done a few things to change the color of my "wallpaper", the background of the phone's screen. I also noticed there was a camera on it, which took pretty good color pictures of my thumb in front of the lens.

"Too complicated," I muttered, as I pocketed the phone when they called my number. I picked up our order and, after waiting a moment, screwed up my courage to go back out into the rain.

"Stop it! You're hurting me!"

"Not as much as I'm gonna hurt you, bitch!"

I froze. The voices were coming from the alleyway next to the restaurant. I heard a thud and a scream.

"Shut up, bitch!"

I wanted to go back to Scott and forget I heard anything — that I didn't hear her muffled scream again, and I didn't hear struggling. I looked skyward, up at the rain, the clouds, then up toward Heaven. "You're testing me, aren't you?"

No response from anyone upstairs. Not even a modest thunderclap.

"Fine," I said, and set the food down in an area where it wouldn't get wet. I turned and headed into the alley.

The man had a girl up against the wall, her arms pinned behind her back. One of the man's hands was free, trying to get her pants off. His pants were already open, exposing himself. The girl — I would say she was 18 or 19 — wore a pair of tight jeans and short shirt, with heels and short fake-red spiky hair. I couldn't see her face, mashed into the brick wall as it was.

"Hey, guy," I called out, giving him a warning. "Pick on someone your own size."

The guy was taller than the girl, built rugged, but fat. His gut hung down, almost covering his penis.

"Mind your own goddamn business," he snapped.

The girl turned her face toward me. She had a bloody nose. Her face was pale. I probably wouldn't be surprised if she had track marks along her arms. *What the hell was I doing?*

"That's my sister," I said.

The girl's eyes widened. The guy threw the girl aside. She stumbled, barely saving herself from smashing her face against a dumpster.

"Your sister's a whore," said the guy.

"Okay, now you've done it," I said, and motioned with my hand. The rain came down in buckets, soaking us both instantly. She probably was a whore. But she didn't need to get beaten up to turn a trick. Even I knew that.

The girl struggled up and ran. The guy buttoned his pants but didn't bother to zip them. He advanced on me, his fists clenched at his sides. He rose them up slowly — a boxer's stance.

From a standing position, without bringing my hands up to defend, I lashed out and punched him in the face.

Pressing 350 was helpful for me, as I broke his nose instantly. He staggered back, his hand to his face. He pulled it away; there was blood on it. Blood also ran down from his nose.

"You little —" he snarled, and charged at me.

I stepped aside, and he continued past me, out of the alley, slamming into a parked car, setting off its alarm. The rain intensified. The Sky Gods found this amusing, it seemed.

The guy turned around and faced me, standing in the mouth of the alleyway, waiting. Some people who were going to merely walk by now stopped underneath the awning of the China Inn, safe from the rain, but watching the fight.

He looked ready to come at me. I stood open, my arms at my sides. Just as he ran at me, I heard a short siren whoop.

The sound distracted me, and he tackled me, throwing me backwards into the alley. I had tried to stay rooted, but he was bigger, slamming into me like a train.

I still was on my feet, though, when I saw two cops come running into the alley behind the guy. His head was pressed against my ribs, and he wrapped his arms around me in an attempt to pick me up and slam me backward onto the pavement.

Mercurius, the wrestler I met in prison who had summoned Baba Yaga to kill soldiers in Bosnia, would have been proud of me as I broke the hold this guy tried to put on me. Of course, the cops helped, peeling the man off me.

In the pouring rain, the man struggled against a cop who stepped between him and me.

"Calm down or we'll put the cuffs on you."

One cop put his hand on my shoulder. "You okay?"

The guy was screaming while he struggled against the other cop. His pants were unbuttoned now, his nether regions exposed for all to see. "He hit me first!"

I nodded to the cop and he let me go. I didn't want to get involved as a victim. It would involve police reports, going down to the station, maybe seeing Ritter, who would say it was my fault, then possibly back to the Rosicrucians for another trial — I didn't need the aggravation.

I stood in the rain while they dragged the guy away from me. No one noticed as I retrieved the food and took the opportunity to walk back to the store.

Scott looked up when I came in. "You're soaking wet."

"I know." I dropped the food onto the counter and fished out his change from my front pocket. Even that was wet.

"Come in the back," he said. "Get out of your wet clothes. You'll catch a cold."

"I can't remember the last time I had a cold," I said. I had used magic to stave off all sorts of sickness that ran through the prison.

The back room was cluttered. A large desk with nothing on it was obviously his main workspace. Shelves that contained herbs and baskets filled up all three walls.

I took off my shirt. He glanced at my chest, blushed, and then took my shirt. He put it on a hanger and hung it up on a rod mounted across the threshold of the back room.

"Pants, too," he said. "I've got a blanket around here." He opened a cupboard and moved some things around, then pulled out a hand-knit afghan. "Here," he said. "Wrap this around you and sit on this chair. Be right back." He headed to the front of the store.

I took off my pants, wrapping the afghan around my waist like a kilt. It came to about my knees. I sat on a folding metal chair.

Scott came back with an electric heater, placed it on the floor in front of me and plugged it in. He turned it on, then grabbed my pants and put them up on the rod, too.

"Thanks," I said.

He brought the food into the back. "You got caught in that downpour?"

"Yeah," I said.

"So," he said, as he put the container of food in front of me. "This question has been bothering me."

"Okay …"

"Why did you summon a demon?"

"Because I got beat up by some kids on the school bus, when someone outed me."

"How did you get outed?"

"One of the boys pretended he wanted to kiss me in gym class. When I got close enough, he screamed and told everyone I tried to kiss him." I waved a hand. "It spread from there. That night I got beat up on the bus home from school."

"Oh, God." Scott stared at me, his eyes wide. "You went home and summoned a demon?"

I nodded. "That night, at midnight, I went in the garage and did the circles there, summoning Belial. My brother had come home late after work. He had somehow found out about me kissing the kid, and he was ready to beat the shit out of me. He didn't even get to the front door."

"What happened?"

"He died in the middle of the lawn. Belial killed him in my name. He killed a lot of people in my name." I paused, and ate a forkful of rice. "The next morning, the Rosicrucians came and pulled me out of my aunt's house, threw me in a van, and drove me to where I later found out was upstate New York, about fifty miles from the Canadian border. The William F. Blackstone prison."

"No trial? No lawyers?"

"My trial was up in New York, where I had to represent myself. I was going to turn 13 in a week. I didn't know what I was doing as a lawyer. They put me in prison until I turned 18. The day after that, I got released."

"Why 18?"

"I'm an adult. I'm considered a rational, thinking being."

"You weren't a rational, thinking being at 13?"

"I was being lead on, they said." I thought of Aunt Jane, how they said she forced me into it, but they should have blamed me entirely.

He frowned. "They didn't contact your parents?"

"They told my parents I ran away and joined a cult. That's what my sister said."

"And now?"

"And now, what?" I asked him.

"Did you tell your parents the truth?"

I shook my head. "I can't tell them the truth. I haven't spoken to them yet because I'm still trying to form my story."

He crossed his arms. "It's better to tell them the truth. Less things to remember and make up."

"They wouldn't believe me. They wouldn't trust me."

"How do you know that?"

"You don't know my father. He'd be angry enough if he knew I was …"

"Gay?" Scott said.

I looked him in the eye. "Yeah."

"He probably already knows," Scott said, turning to look down at his congealed beef and broccoli. "My parents knew."

"They did? What happened?"

He sighed. "They sent me off to boarding school. They weren't very supportive. They thought military boarding school would beat it out of me. It didn't. I jumped a few grades and graduated early. Then I took the money they had for me in trust and opened up this shop. I don't make enough money to pay the rent, but it's something I always wanted to do."

"Do you talk to them?"

"Only on holidays. I don't bring over my boyfriends, so they don't ask about it. They think I own a regular bookstore."

I reached over and placed my hand on top of his. He looked down at my hand. I waited for the door outside to open. "As soon as I get some money," I said, "you and I are going on a date."

He smiled. "I thought this was one?"

"I usually don't take my pants off on the first date."

He laughed.

I ate a little of the coagulated gravy on top of the egg patty. "So your parents are rich?"

"So-so? They have enough to have a house in the Florida Keys and Newport. And they run in the social circles of both places."

"You have brothers and sisters?"

"No, I'm their only child." He took down a hotplate and kettle from one of the shelves. "Tea?"

"Sure," I said.

He went out of the room, to a door that was blocked by a set of shelves on wheels. He pushed the shelves aside and ducked into what looked to me like a broom closet, but was a tiny bathroom. I heard running water, and then he came back with a full kettle. He set it on the hotplate and turned it on.

I ate a little of the cold food. "Was anyone supportive?"

"If you believe it, the kids at school were. As long as I didn't talk about it, they treated me like everyone else. In fact, there were a few other kids like me."

"But the teachers?"

"Oh, no," he said. "No support there."

I ate. It was gross. I put it aside, finally.

"Don't like it?"

"It's cold. Are my clothes dry yet?"

"Are you kidding?"

"Can I have my pants? I'll at least warm them up."

He chuckled and got up, then pulled my pants from the hanger. I put them up against the heater, being careful not to set them on fire. Just as Scott sat back down, the door opened out front. He looked at his food, closed up the box, and turned to the store.

"Oh, hey," he said.

"Hey," said Bennett. "What's up?"

"Just waiting for Mike to dry out."

"Is he drunk?"

Scott laughed. "No, he's soaked from being out in the rain."

"I don't like drinking," I called out.

"Ah, a teetotaler." Bennett came into view, standing in the doorway next to Scott. "I got another job yesterday." He looked at the afghan wrapped around my legs. "Nice skirt."

"Gee," I said with a grin. "Thanks."

"Anyway. Some woman is cheating on her husband. Care to join me on this excursion?"

I admit it; I whined. "Do I have to?"

"I thought you wanted to get into the private eye business? Can't you do some mumbo-jumbo to follow someone?"

"I can't do too much 'mumbo-jumbo' as you call it, because I'm on probation of sorts."

I felt my drying pants. They were warm, but still wet.

"I have to head home," I told Scott. I let the afghan drop. The side that exposed my boxers was opposite Scott. He looked away anyway. I pulled on my pants, even as Bennett watched.

"I'll give you a ride. It's raining buckets outside."

"Thanks, I appreciate it." I pulled on my very cold, wet shirt, and my nipples hardened beneath. Scott looked right at them. There was no way he couldn't see them.

He looked up at me, and he blushed. "Sorry, I —"

"It's okay," I said, giving him a warm smile. "It's not the first time someone stared."

He turned away from me, going out to the store.

I looked up at Bennett. "What? What did I say?"

"C'mon," Bennett grumbled, heading to the door.

I looked back at Scott, but he wasn't looking at me. Instead, he straightened some shelves that didn't need straightening. I left, going out into the rain. I ran to Bennett's car and struggled to shut the door. "Wha'd I say?"

"You don't have to be such a dick," Bennett said, "about how you look."

"All I said was —"

"He likes you," Bennett snapped.

I opened my mouth, then closed it. "How can you tell?" I asked quietly.

Bennett started up the car. "You've got a lot to learn, kid."

I was confused. Really, what had I said that was so wrong? I started to shiver, Bennett put on the heat as the car grew foggy inside.

"So about that guy, any idea where he might be?" he asked.

"None."

"Any idea why he would have summoned the demon in the first place?"

"Could be anything, Frank. I know he used his own blood combined with that of an animal." Otherwise I wouldn't be able to see him in my mind's eye when I did that spell," I mused aloud. "If he used an animal's blood, then that means that the demon isn't necessarily tied to him."

"What do you mean?"

"I mean that he might not be possessed. It might have possessed someone else. I wonder what vessel he did put Belial in. Unless …"

"Unless?"

"He set him loose."

"So Belial is just walking around in the world."

"Put simply, yes."

Bennett drummed his fingers on the steering wheel as we waited for a light to change. "So how do we send the demon back?"

"Well, one way is to wait for him to do something."

"Like what?"

"Most likely kill somebody."

"So we what, wait for another body to show up?"

"It depends what he summoned Belial for. I still don't know that."

"It's what you'd summon Belial for, right? To kill someone?"

"Yes, but the guy … he was a business man. A little nerdy. It could be that he wants his business to take off. Or even to go after a boss." Someone drove by us and splashed us with rain. His windshield wipers cleared it away. "I really need to know why he summoned him."

We got to Dom and Evie's apartment. Their car was in the driveway.

"Hey, thanks for giving me a ride," I said.

"No problem. You get any other ideas, let me know. I'll let my contacts know at the station."

I nodded and ducked out into the rain.

CHAPTER TEN

SPIRITS

I ENTERED THE APARTMENT MY TEETH CHATTERING. Dom was inside, where it was nice and warm, at the computer. He glanced at me when I came in.

"You okay?"

"I'm freezing," I said. "I'm going to take a hot shower."

"Okay," he said, and turned back to the computer.

I stripped down and jumped into the hot shower. I felt better, but I started feeling weak. I hadn't eaten. Maybe that was it.

After the shower, though, I couldn't warm up. I shivered constantly, even as I sipped hot tea and lay on the couch, wrapped in two blankets and clothed in a sweatshirt and sweatpants.

"You caught yourself a cold," Dom said, after he pushed away from the computer. "I have to go get Evie." He patted Rufus. "I'll take you out when I get home."

Evie came home and, like a good mom, she felt my forehead. "You're warm," she said. "Let me get the thermometer."

Her thermometer was a thing that she stuck in my ear, not the old-fashioned stick-this-glass-tube-under-your-tongue. She placed it in my ear and, after a few seconds, it beeped.

"It's a little high: 99. I'd keep you home tomorrow if it's over 100."

"Yes, mom," I said with a gentle smile.

She smiled back, then rustled up a can of chicken noodle soup. I ate it sitting at the kitchen counter, still wrapped up in blankets.

The next day I was miserable. Coughing, sneezing, runny nose — the whole shebang. I hadn't had a cold in six years, and had forgotten how it felt. I didn't like it. It took all my strength to get up, go to the bathroom, and then go back to the couch. Dom avoided me like I had the plague, while Evie sprayed Lysol everywhere.

During that day, and the weekend that followed, I read and pondered. TV news didn't have anything about the ritual found in the woods. Bennett didn't call me. Neither did Scott.

On Monday, I felt a lot better and went with Dom to bring Evie to the school. We were halfway home when she called Dom. I answered the phone while he was driving.

"Hey, Mike, I forgot my bag with my lesson plan and everything. Can you get it and bring it to me?"

"Sure," I said, and relayed the message to Dom.

He grumbled, but we went back to the house. "I'm going to the Y after this," he said. "If you're up to coming."

"Yep," I said.

I went upstairs, grabbed my gym bag and Evie's bag, and dashed downstairs to the car. Dom was listening to the news on the radio when I got downstairs. I knew he was a news junkie — it comes from being a reporter, I guess.

We got to the school, and I got out.

"I'll bring this to her," I said to him. "I'll walk to the Y from here." This time I'd checked the forecast: sunny, low 70's.

Dom nodded. It was only about a mile to downtown. He took off as I went through the front door of the school. The door in the foyer was open, even though it said to push a button to talk to someone to come in. I walked up two steps and looked around for the office. I found it on my left.

I went inside, and didn't see anyone at the counter. In fact, I saw no one inside. I called out, "Hello?"

I heard a moan.

I pushed open the waist-high, double-swinging half-door that separated where I stood from the other side of the counter, and walked cautiously around it. A woman lay there in a pool of blood that flowed from her head. I tilted my body to look behind another desk. Another woman was stretched out on the floor, blood expanding in a widening circle beneath her.

I picked up the phone at the nearest desk and called 9-1-1.

"What is your emergency?" answered the woman.

"I'm in the main office of the school, and I see two people dead."

Someone was calling via the intercom from another room. "Mary?"

"Dead?" asked the dispatcher.

"Shot, I think."

The intercom went off again, "Mary, are you there?"

"Please stay on the line, sir. How many people are dead?"

"I see two. Wait …" I started to go around the corner of another desk, but the phone's cord wouldn't let me. I could see another person's legs and more blood. "Three. And there's another office I can't get to."

"Stay where you are, sir."

The intercom was on the other side of the room. I put the phone down and went over to it. After looking it over, I didn't know where the button was to respond back.

A kid came in. "Where's Mrs. Miller?"

"Busy," I said. I couldn't let him come around the corner.

Then I heard firecrackers. But I knew they weren't firecrackers.

"Oh, no," I said, and rushed around the counter, forgetting about the open phone line on the desk. The kid stared at me as I grabbed him by the shoulders and guided him out.

"Where's your class?"

A door opened and Evie stepped out into the hallway. Another door opened and a man stepped out too.

"What's going on?" he asked.

Evie came over and took the child from me. "Mike, somebody was yelling. I think it came from Patricia's room."

"Shit." I heard the sirens. I thrust the little boy at her. "Take him, where's Patricia's room?"

"Don't go there, Mike!" But I started walking down the hall anyway.

Another door opened, and I saw a man standing in the doorway, holding the hand of a crying little girl. Open wounds covered his face, as if he'd had extra-large pimples that had all burst. His eyes were wild, wide and darting from place to place. He held a handgun.

"Get back!" I yelled at Evie, as the man raised the gun.

Evie screamed as the man pulled the trigger.

Click.

I almost pissed my pants. Instead, I ran at the man, tackling him, throwing him into the side of the doorway. The gun went flying. The little girl broke away to run into the hallway.

The man was strong, even though he looked weak, covered in pus-filled wounds. He tried to bite my face. I pulled back, holding him in place with one hand on his shoulder. He roared at me like an animal, his hands clawing at my arm. He drew blood. I kept my arm straight out, not moving, as I held him hard against the wall.

Then he tried to kick me. He aimed for my knee, but I moved out of the way, going off balance. He scrambled out from under me and ran out into the hallway, right into a gauntlet of four police officers.

I dove to the floor when I saw that all four cops had pulled their guns. All four fired at him at close range. He went down face-first, like a bull under an onslaught of swords.

Then I watched as he pressed his hands on against the floor, pushing himself up. He had been shot in the head, so the left side of it was missing. The cops backed up. The man got to his feet again, dripping blood where he stood.

I took a wild guess. "Belial!"

He paused, and then slowly turned to me. His face was covered in blood. One eye was gone, the other eye a clear blue, almost bugging out of his face. He grinned, white teeth shining under black blood.

"Boy wizard," he said, his voice thick and full of fluid.

"Leave them alone," I demanded. "Leave that vessel."

"Do you think you can command me?" he roared. "You, a mere boy wizard?"

The cops had reloaded, but couldn't shoot because I was in their way.

"Move out of the way," yelled one of them.

But the wounded man shuffled toward me. The little girl was screaming "Daddy!", while Evie held her back.

"You can be my vessel, Wizard," said the man, still grinning. "Together, we can rule this world."

"Until you use me up. No, no thank you."

"It is because of this vessel. It is weak. You are strong."

I hesitated. It was tempting. Then I looked at Evie. I couldn't let her down. My hand made a sign of protection. Belial hissed at me. Then he turned, lightning-fast, and ran at the cops again.

The officers yelled something, I don't know what, while I dove again to the side, flattening myself against one of the classroom doors to make myself as small of a target as I could. I felt a bullet graze my nose, but my protection spell held. I turned to face the hallway after the gunfire ended. Smoke drifted through the hallway; a thick scent of iron hung in the air.

The man was face-down again, maybe for the count this time. Evie had disappeared, though I could hear the little girl screaming through a door. I put my hands out in an attempt to feel if the spirit had left the body and now wandered freely. One of the cops, a brave one, went up to the body. He bent down as the rest of the cops advanced, guns drawn on the body. The brave cop poked at the body. It didn't move.

One of the four officers called to me. "Hey, is he dead?"

"I don't see or sense him," I replied. Like trying to read the dirt, reading the air was not my thing. I was afraid if I opened myself up, that Belial would jump right in and take me over. If he was in the area, it would be too late for me to stop him.

They put handcuffs on what was left of the guy on the floor anyway.

"We gotta get the kids outta here," said the brave cop. He turned to the others. "Get a blanket from outside. Paul, start clearing out the kids through the back door."

There were two doors at two stairwells on either side of the building. The cops separated and started escorting the kids out the farthest end after we had covered the body and the area.

I stood next to the body. The blankets turned black as they soaked up the blood. I smelled the decay of the body, the iron of the blood. Paramedics came in and started to clear out the bodies from the office.

A cop pulled out the man's wallet. "Darryl Johnson," he said, looking up at me. I shook my head. He went through the man's wallet, pawing through his credit cards and other assorted items. I saw a school picture of the little girl who had been screaming.

Paramedics then went into Patricia's room. They came out with two small bodies and a large one.

"Shit," I whispered, watching the large one go down the corridor.

The kids in that room had been escorted out by one of the other teachers. I could only imagine the trauma.

I went outside to find Evie with her kids. Parents were running up, grabbing their kids, and whisking them away. No one was taking charge. No one counted the kids. No one was stopping the parents.

"I gotta go to the bathroom," said one little boy to me, holding his groin and bowing up and down. I looked helplessly at one of the teachers, who took the little boy's free hand and brought him back into the building. Another teacher stepped in to gather up the remaining kids.

One parent started screaming at a teacher. "You people need to put in metal detectors! You people need to have ways of stopping people like this from coming into school! You people can't —"

I wanted to walk over and tell her to shut up, but one of the cops ended up coming over and escorting the shouting woman away. The teacher broke down and started to cry. The little girls tried to comfort her; the little boys looked uncomfortable. The teacher from the bathroom returned and went over to the woman who sat on the ground, crying.

I stood near Evie as her kids as their parents peeled them off, one by one. A bus showed up around noon to pick up the rest. Some kids wanted to go back in for their lunches or their homework, but no one was allowed back inside.

"Mike," Evie finally asked me, after all of the kids had been boarded onto busses and only the teachers remained. "Did you know him?"

"No."

"You called him Belial."

"Because he had that demon in him. It was a guess."

Evie's eyes welled up with tears. "Patricia ..."

"Yes."

"Mikey —" she said, and threw her arms around my neck. I hugged her tight.

"I won't let anything happen to you," I said. She hugged me fiercely and sobbed quietly.

A cop came over to us. "Excuse me," he said.

I turned to look at him. It was the brave cop who had gone up to the body. The name on his uniform said Cabral.

"Hi," I said, as Evie pulled back, wiping her eyes and face.

"I'm sorry." She sniffled.

"It's all right, ma'am," he said. "You okay?"

"Yeah," we both said.

Cabral turned to me. "Can we speak with you?"

"Sure," I replied. I went with him to a guy in a suit. My stomach flittered; it must be a detective. The guy had the same attitude that Hotchkiss did: casual but wary.

"Here he is," Cabral said, by way of introduction.

The detective was Hispanic, dark hair and eyes, dark skin. He was maybe in his early 40's, had a small paunch, and spoke with a lilting accent. He nodded to me. "What's your name?"

"Michael LeBonte," I told him.

"Did you know the suspect?"

"No."

"They said you called his name."

"He was possessed."

The detective raised an eyebrow. "Possessed."

"Possessed by Belial. A demon of Hell."

"You expect me to believe that?"

"What did the cops tell you?"

"They said you called his name."

"The name of the spirit who possessed him."

"Are you a priest?"

"No. I'm a wizard."

He looked at me like I was insane. "What did you call him?"

"Belial."

"Why?"

I sighed. "I told you. He was possessed by the demon Belial."

He crossed his arms. "Let's go down to the station."

"Do I have to?"

"No," he said. "Not yet."

He was just as bad as Ritter. "Look," I said. "Talk to Hotchkiss." His eyes widened a little. "Tell him I work with Frank Bennett. He'll remember me."

"Sure," he said. "You can go."

I frowned and turned away, heading back to Evie. She was standing with three teachers, who were just standing together, not saying anything. I stopped within her line of sight. She broke from the group and came over to me.

"You okay, Evie?"

"My professors never said anything about someone coming in to shoot up the building," she said, forcing a laugh. "It's since Columbine."

"Since who?"

"Columbine. You were probably in prison when it happened. Some kids with guns went into a high school in Colorado and started shooting." She looked back at the doorway. "I'll have to get my things tomorrow," she said. "Dom's on his way."

Evie and I waited in the schoolyard. Finally, we saw the green Camry drive by. Dom couldn't pull into the parking lot, so he parked in front of the school. We went around the yard and walked down the sidewalk. Dom got out of the car and ran up to Evie, throwing his arms around her and pulling her into a fierce embrace.

"Jesus Christ, Evie. Are you okay?"

She started to cry again. I stepped back from them, giving them space. Dom hugged her until she pushed him away gently.

"I'm okay," she said, sniffing.

"I heard about it on the news, but the traffic here was crazy. They blocked off the street."

"It's okay. I'm okay. But Patricia ..." she looked at me. I looked down. "I'll tell you about it later. I just want to go home."

Dom nodded, and the three of us went to the car. As soon as we got in, though, she started telling Dom what had happened. He went into journalist mode, asking questions, prompting her to continue. I silently looked out the window. She explained from her point of view, leaving me out of it. She kept saying "we," like, "We saved the little girl."

"Who's we?"

"Me and Mike."

"Mike?" Dom looked at me through the rear-view mirror. "Were you there too?"

I sighed. "No comment."

"C'mon, man," said Dom. "This could be my big break!"

"Do I have to be named?"

"Well, yeah."

I shook my head. "No. I won't say anything because —"

"Dammit!" Dom said, stopped the car, and whirled around in his seat. "You stay in our house, eat our food, the least you could do is earn your keep."

I backed further into the seat. "Okay. Okay, I'll give you an interview when we get home."

"Dom," said Evie, putting a hand on his arm.

Dom turned to Evie, didn't apologize to me, threw the car into drive, and started down the street.

Dom slammed the newspaper down on the counter. The look on his face didn't seem very happy. Evie was still sleeping. It was Saturday, so things were going to be kind of slow around here.

I gave Rufus a treat, then I asked Dom, "What's wrong?"

"After all that I got out of you last night, you know what I get?" He folded the paper and showed it to me. It took me a minute to find what he was pointing out. On page three, continuing the story from page one, after the last paragraph was a single italicized statement, *"With reporting from Andre Pepard, Dominic Marcello, and AP reports."*

I looked up at him. His Italian temper revealed itself with his red face and a pulsing vein on his forehead.

"Can you believe this? Not even a god damn byline!" He tore the paper out of my hands and slammed it down again.

Finally, he calmed down enough so that his face was no longer red.

I changed subjects. "Are you going to the Y?" I asked him.

"I guess so," he said, still angry. "At least that's *some* place that appreciates me."

A little while later, I left with Dom for the Y. This time, I got my workout and swim in. Afterward, I went upstairs to the TV room. The lights were off, and there were couches and chairs set up all around a large-screen projection TV. I went inside the darkened room and sat in one of the chairs. I assumed my meditative stance, feet flat on the ground, hands on my thighs, sitting straight up. My body slipped into trance immediately.

Too afraid to leave the body, I instead did a body scan. Nothing hurt, really. I saw the lights go on behind my lids, and heard a man's sharp, "Oh!"

I slipped open my eyes and turned my head. Max stood in the doorway. "I'm sorry," he said. "I didn't realize you were here."

"It's all right." I got up and stretched. "My ride might be ready by now."

"Was that meditating?"

I nodded.

"I thought you sat in one of those lotus positions and say 'ommmmm.'"

I laughed. "No, this is an easier position if you're not flexible. And you say 'Ohm' only to distract yourself."

"You should teach a class here on meditating. I'll bet people would come."

"I'm not that good at teaching," I said. I really didn't think I could do that.

"I'd go," said Max. "Lord knows I need to calm down. Been at it for a while?"

"Just over three years," I said. "That and weight training is all I concentrated on."

"Did you have to go on a protein diet or something?"

"I went on a diet," I said quietly. A forced diet, the worst food in the world compared to what was out here.

He nodded. "I gotta stop going to the Chinese buffet." He patted his flat abs.

I laughed again. "I'll be seeing you, Max. If you want help on what to do with weights and stuff, I can help you out with that."

"Sure, man." He waved goodbye, and I heard his phone go off, gentle little tones.

I went downstairs to the office.

"Dom?"

"Yeah!" he called. "Almost done here. Gah! Stupid Microsoft!"

Out in the main lobby, a very dark-skinned boy stood waiting. I saw a man walk by and stare at the boy, then he stopped and walked up to him. I was just beyond the doorway of the lobby, so the man couldn't see me.

"Hey," he said to the boy. "Are you waiting for someone?"

"My dad," he said.

"Where is he?"

The boy nodded. He looked about 8 or 9, his head shaved bald, with deep, soulful black eyes. The man who loomed over him was about my age, maybe a little older, thinner than me. I couldn't see his face immediately.

"Want to come back with me and we'll go find him?"

"He told me to wait here."

The man got really close to the boy. I watched warily.

"It won't take long. We can search for him together."

The boy was wise. He backed up away from the man. That's when I stepped into the room.

The man turned to me, surprised. I had seen things like this happen in prison. More than once, I had been the victim of it.

As I watched the man, he now moved away from the boy.

"Can I help you?" I asked, with my most dazzling smile.

"Just leaving," said the man, who looked every inch a weasel.

Max was coming up the stairs, on a phone.

"Yeah, yeah. I'll be there in half an hour. Have to drop off Deacon. Right. I know —" He stopped short in front of me. "I've gotta go," he said, as the boy went over to Max. "Everything okay?"

"Is now," I said.

Deacon nodded. Max put a hand on the boy's shoulder. "Let's go," he said. Just as Max went out of the glass doors of the Y, Dom came out of the director's office.

"Okay, Mike. Hungry?"

"No wieners."

He laughed. "No wieners," he agreed. "How about pizza?"

I smiled. "Sure."

My week went like that. I went to the Y four times that week. Dom, even though he was furious at the fact he didn't get a byline, still drove around the northern part of the state collecting stories. We settled into a routine.

On Sunday, when we had to pay the rent, the landlord bumped it up another $35 because I was staying there. Dom shut up and paid the extra money. We had enough money left over to get two pizzas.

Monday morning, I had planned on going out to the gym, but I found Bennett waiting outside as we were leaving. He looked tired, like he had just rolled out of bed.

"Morning," he said to us, as we walked down the little walkway to the car.

"Morning," said Dom.

"What's up?" I asked him.

Bennett looked directly at me. "The cops need a magician."

"Sure," I said. I gave Evie a kiss goodbye on her cheek and followed Bennett to his car. "What's going on?"

"I'm not sure myself," he said, "But it's not pretty. Have you ever been around dead bodies before?"

"I watched them kill that guy in the school," I said. I didn't feel apprehensive or scared. I struggled with the door as he turned the key.

"Great. Just don't get sick."

"What's going on, Frank?"

He shook his head. "Weird shit. Even Hotchkiss doesn't know what to make of it. Did you hear the news this morning?"

"No," I said.

We headed away from Pawtucket and instead headed south, toward Providence. He put on the radio and fell silent. It was talk radio, news stuff, local stuff that I didn't care about. I tuned it out, like I did when Dom listened to it. Then Bennett said, "There."

"—ucket police officer shot and killed his wife and daughter in their home, then turned the gun on himself. Police are investigating. In national news …"

"A Pawtucket cop?" I said, faking that I heard the whole thing.

"Yeah. What they aren't telling you is what he did to them first, at least according to the ME."

"ME?"

"Medical Examiner. And Aaron. Hotchkiss. He went there because he's the highest-ranking detective on the force. He was disturbed enough by what he saw for me to call you."

"What does a cop shooting have to do with me?"

Bennett shrugged. "Aaron was spooked by something. Since you're on the payroll, you're the go-to guy for spooky shit."

I looked out the window.

We drove past Providence, getting off the highway in Warwick. We ended up in front of a glass and steel building that looked like a giant had sat on it, turning it from an elegant six-story building to a squat and wide three-floor one. We went inside.

Cops lined the hallways, both Pawtucket and Providence cops. We went down two flights of stairs; the air became cold and brittle. I shivered and hunkered into my borrowed hoodie.

Walking down an antiseptic and pristine white hallway, the sound of our footsteps echoed off the walls. It was a morgue, I realized, looking through a window as we passed it. Cabinet doors filled one wall in that room. I counted eight by three doors along its wall.

I turned to see Hotchkiss and his partner standing just outside another room.

"Morning. Glad you could make it, " Hotchkiss said. He tilted his head toward the doorway. "First time you been in a place like this?"

It felt like prison, but white instead of gray. "Yes and no," I said. "I've never been in a morgue."

"Ever seen a dead body?"

"Other than the ones they shot in the school? No."

"How'd you handle that?"

"I don't have nightmares." Though I could pull up the whole thing again in my head, as clear as if it was happening right in front of me now.

"That's a positive note," he said. "Okay. We're gonna have to take a chance." He opened the door. The stench of antiseptic filled my nostrils. It felt ice-cold inside here. I zipped up the hoodie and followed Hotchkiss inside.

A body lay on a metal table — or something covered with a sheet. It must have been a body, because nothing else had quite that kind of a shape. I focused on it as we walked forward.

Hotchkiss turned and looked at me. "You sure you're going to be okay?"

I nodded. The smell was getting to me, though.

Hotchkiss pulled on a pair of latex gloves and turned down the sheet. It was the brave cop from the shooting, the one who had poked the body and who asked me to talk to the other detective. His face was pale and clean-shaven. His eyes were closed. His hair was matted, however, with dark stuff that I assumed was blood.

"I need you to come close," Hotchkiss told me.

He stank of old blood, antiseptic, and alcohol — and a sweet decaying smell that almost turned my stomach. I swallowed and stepped forward. Hotchkiss was digging his hands in the hair just above the man's forehead. He parted it for me to see something.

I saw a small black pointy piece of bone. That was on one side, parallel to his eye. On the other side was the same thing. Hotchkiss said, "Is that what I think it is?"

"Devil horns? Yes, I think so."

"Sweet baby Jesus," said Bennett in the kind of tone that I figured he might have made the sign of the cross, like Dom did — unless he wasn't Catholic.

"How long would he have been possessed for something like this to happen?" Hotchkiss pulled the sheet back over body.

I backed away.

"I don't know," I said, looking down at the body. "This is the first time I've ever seen a physical manifestation of a demon on a person." This was so out of my league, but I didn't dare tell him that.

"Was he even possessed?" asked Bennett.

Hotchkiss looked up at Bennett for a half-minute. "Once the ME showed me this, it's what I thought."

Hotchkiss then looked at me while he took off the gloves. I had stepped back, making sure that I wouldn't fall back, although I really did want to get out of there. Hotchkiss didn't seem to be in any hurry, though.

"How did you know Belial was there?"

"I guessed."

"Did he talk to you?"

I could still hear that voice. Did I want to rule the world? Tempting as it was, I knew darn well that I wouldn't stop him from taking me over. I'd probably go right back to the prison and raze it to the ground, destroying the Templars and their holier-than-thou bull. But my vessel would be temporary, just like the guy at the school had been, and just like this guy was.

"Yes," I said to Hotchkiss. "Yes, he talked to me. He tempted me."

"Because that's what the devil does. He probably tempted Russ." Hotchkiss walked around the body. "So what happened to the spirit?"

"Where there any survivors?"

"Not in his house," Hotchkiss gestured toward the body.

"I'm including the cat. Or dog. Or even fish."

Hotchkiss raised an eyebrow. "Dog? I think he had a dog …"

"That could be a temporary vessel until he gets back into a human."

"How does the devil get into a human?"

"You have to want it."

"Jesus Christ," said Bennett. "How do we stop it?"

"Perform an exorcism. Or a banishment. But the vessel could die if I do that."

Hotchkiss left the room to a doorway down the hall.

"Stu? We're done." He returned to us, and then we walked down the hall to where the cops were gathered. "Did he have a dog, or a cat, anyone know?"

"Had a dog named Randy," said one of the cops.

"Find that dog."

I was a little hesitant, but I asked anyway: "Um, Detective?"

He turned to me. "Yeah?"

"Have the Animal Control Officer, if he's Catholic, wear a crucifix? Or a rosary."

Hotchkiss did not look at me like I was crazy. Instead, he just nodded. Hotchkiss told the cops, "Anybody goes into that house, get a rosary. Get it blessed for good measure."

The cops looked at each other. I'm sure they were thinking I was crazy. Hotchkiss walked through the gauntlet of cops. Bennett and I followed him; the cops fell in behind us. I wanted to explain that the magic wasn't in the rosary, but in the intent of it. If the cops believed that it protected them, then the rosary would work. If they thought it was bunk, then it wouldn't.

Hotchkiss got outside and turned around to face us again. "You be ready to do a banishment," he told me "What do you need?"

"I, um, I have to look it up. But I'm sort of on probation and not allowed to."

"Probation officer?" He stopped while the cops continued past us.

"You know about the Rosicrucians, right?"

Hotchkiss's eyes widened slightly. "You ran into them?"

"A few years back."

Hotchkiss frowned for a minute, and I thought he was going to tell me to leave and never come back. Instead, he did something surprising. "You tell your probation officer to talk to me," he said firmly. "When can you get what you need?"

I didn't think Scott would have a copy of the *Greater Key of Solomon*. "I think I have to go to Salem."

Hotchkiss nodded. He looked at Bennett, who was behind me. I couldn't see Bennett's reaction.

"We'll find that dog and then you do that banishment on that dog."

"Sure," I said to his back, as he turned and headed to his car.

Bennett put a hand on my shoulder. "Do you need a ride to Salem?"

"I'm going to, yeah. I'm supposed to meet Dom at the Y because he has the car."

"Call him," said Bennett. "I'll bring you to Salem now."

CHAPTER ELEVEN

PREPARATIONS

WE DROVE WITH THE WINDOWS DOWN so I could try to get the stench of the morgue out of my nose. D'Luna's store was closed, and wouldn't be open for another hour, so Bennett offered to buy me breakfast at a diner down the road from the witchy shops. We sat at the counter, and I satisfied myself with eggs, home fries, and toast. Bennett had a huge breakfast which consisted of the same thing as mine did, plus a whole lot more.

We hadn't spoken much on the way. I was occupied with my thoughts, mostly of the banishment ritual as I remembered it. I had performed it only once, without a vessel, to be rid of Andromalius, the first demon I had summoned when I was 11. I did it to punish a boy named Mousey who had beat me up since second grade. Andromalius killed another boy, and I had to banish him before he killed again. Luckily, the Templars hadn't caught me that time.

I was concerned with the Templars. What if Ritter found out I was getting myself a *Key of Solomon* book? What if he knew I was going to be doing a ritual? Did Hotchkiss hold sway over the Templars?

Bennett sopped up his eggs with his toast and said, "Do you know what you're doing, Mike?"

"Sure," I said, with much more confidence than I actually felt. "I've done this before."

"How many times?"

"Once."

Bennett frowned. "That's great."

"It's not hard," I said. Though it was harder to banish than it was to summon — at least I thought so. It was like getting rid of a trusted weapon. It was useful, maybe to you, but dangerous to keep in plain sight. "It's all in the intent."

"You gotta wanna," said Bennett. He picked up a napkin and wiped his mouth. "He should be open now."

We went to D'Luna's store, and it was open. The leftover scent of patchouli still hung in the air. The girl who had been with him when I saw him at the summoning area stood behind the counter. She looked at me like she didn't recognize me.

"Can I help you?"

"I'm looking for the *Key of Solomon*."

She pointed to the books shelved against one wall. I went over to them, and saw all sorts of books on Wicca and paganism. Then, out of order, I found it: the *Key of Solomon*. My heart gave a little leap.

"Hello, old friend," I said, plucking it from the bookcase. I turned to Bennett. "Who's paying for all this?"

Bennett sighed. "I guess I will. Get Hotchkiss to reimburse me."

"Ah, so you're back," I heard D'Luna's voice call to me.

I knew D'Luna would be there, but I had planned for this contingency by not turning around to face him. "I need a few things."

He snorted. "What makes you think I even have them?"

I held up the book.

"Everybody on this street has a copy of that."

"Then I should be able to get what I need from everybody. But I wanted to stop here, first."

"Whatever for? To rub in the fact that you took one of my clients away?"

He held his arms crossed in the ancient gesture of putting up a wall against me. I could tell from his stance that he wasn't going to open up to me.

"I need the implements for a banishment ritual."

`Belial," he said.

I nodded.

"He's not going to be that easy to get rid of."

"I know."

"You will have to have a full coven to perform the banishing ritual."

I shook my head. "I don't want a full coven, because then he can just jump into another vessel. Anyone there who has any inkling of wanting power and glory, he'll go right to them."

"Where is he right now?"

"I think in a dog."

D'Luna looked down his nose at me. "You think?"

"I can't read spirits in vessels."

"But I can." He straightened his head, so that he was looking directly at me. "It sounds like you need some help."

"I don't need any help," I said.

Bennett piped in. "Maybe you should."

Whose side was he on? I turned to him, but D'Luna spoke, "I'll give you what you need, provided we work together on this."

"I can do this by myself." I looked from Bennett to D'Luna. "I've banished a demon before."

"Who?" asked D'Luna.

"Andromalius."

"A lesser demon who wouldn't mind going back to Hell," D'Luna said with a dismissive wave of his hand. "You're dealing with Belial now, a duke with legions of demons at his command. If he succeeds in staying out of Hell, then who knows what will follow him."

"I didn't think of that," said Bennett.

D'Luna talked directly to Bennett now. "It may start the Apocalypse, when God will send his angels down to defeat the demons, and there will be an all-out war in this world." He turned to face me now. "You never found the man who summoned Belial?"

"No," I said, trying hard not to hunch up my shoulders and look sheepish.

D'Luna sighed melodramatically. "Again, you should have asked for my help. I would have been able to find him."

"You didn't even know that was Belial's sigil on the ground!"

"I don't traffic in demons." He studied me. "I don't summon them, and I don't often banish them. Not many people are as crazy as you, summoning demons from the *Greater Key of Solomon.*"

"Somebody else was," Bennett said. "Mike, I think you should take help when it's offered."

I held the book tightly. Bennett, I suppose, was right, but I didn't want to admit it. I knew I could do it by myself. In fact, how would I know if D'Luna was doing this just to get at Belial, and possibly get the demon for himself? If he was as powerful a witch as he presented himself to be, then he would want Belial to augment his powers, for certain.

"I don't know when they're going to call me," I said to D'Luna.

"I've been on call for them before."

"I suppose you'll expect a cut."

He shrugged. "I'll do this *pro bono*."

"You'll want a favor later."

"I may ask you for a favor, but as a colleague."

"Yeah. Right."

Bennett looked like he was ready to hit me. "Mike, c'mon. Stop being a dick."

"He's afraid I'll steal the glory," D'Luna said. "I promise not to."

"I'm more afraid you're going to screw it up somehow," I pointed out. "You said you don't traffic in demons."

D'Luna threw up his hands. "Why do I even bother?" He turned from us and started back toward the counter.

That's when Bennett slapped me on the back of the head. "Mike, are you an idiot?"

I know I gave him an angry look. "He'll screw it up, I know he will."

"You're jealous."

"I am not!"

"I can tell jealous," Bennett said. "This guy is offering to help. He's done work for the police before. You haven't. He's done this kind of thing before too. You've done it only once. There's nothing wrong with learning from people who know more than you."

I stood there, holding the book like it was a lifeline. I had learned stuff in prison from people who knew more than me and, back then, I wasn't as ... what? Proud? I knew things that others didn't know; that was true. But in prison, there were so many wizards and witches that knew more than me, and I had sat at their feet to listen to their wisdom. Coming out into the real world, among the mundanes who didn't know magic, I felt like I was a god among men.

Hubris, they called it. Fate always stepped in to straighten your ass out when you started getting that attitude.

"D'Luna!" I called.

He turned back to me as he stood behind the counter. "What?"

"I accept your offer."

"Now say you're sorry, Mike," prompted Bennett.

"Sorry? For what?" I whirled around on Bennett.

D'Luna waved a hand. "Forget it. I'm not going to get an apology out of him." He leaned on the counter. "What do you need?"

"Everything. Chalice. Lighters. Incense, candles. Chalk. Salt. Knife —"

"Give me the book."

I handed it to him. He broke the plastic seal encasing the book and paged through it. "There's not much in here by way of dismissals," he said.

"I banished Andromalius." But I had used a ritual in the *Key of Solomon* — or was it something that I'd made up?

"Was Andromalius in a creature?"

"No. No, he was a free spirit."

D'Luna regarded me. "That's impossible."

"No, it's not," I said. I had pointed this out to one of the wizards in prison once, and got into a heated argument. He was of the same opinion as D'Luna, that demons needed a physical vessel. "He did what I commanded and returned to me."

"Do you know how dangerous that is, setting a spirit loose like that?"

"I know now." Then, when I had summoned Andromalius and Belial, they didn't seem to want to possess me. They did what I wanted, and that's all I had cared about.

D'Luna only shook his head. "Virgin parchment, robes — I don't have this on such a short demand."

"We don't need robes. I did it in street clothes."

"Robes conduct the energy better."

"But pants are just fine …"

"Look," said Bennett. "If you're going to argue about what clothes you're going to wear, I'm going to go down the street and find out if I can get the shit we need without the debate."

"You need proper implements," D'Luna said.

"Just the basics," I retorted.

"What're you, a poor man's version of a wizard?"

I leaned on the counter menacingly, "Look. I had to do all my work without my parents knowing about it. I had to pack everything I needed in a backpack that I could take in and out of the woods. My Aunt Jane was the one who taught me. She didn't have the space to do a lot of the rituals, so we had to hide in parks and woods. We took over spaces that we had to consecrate before every ritual, because kids used it for their drinking and their bonfires. So don't tell me everything has to be perfect to get this right, because I know that it doesn't have to be."

D'Luna had backed up, as I expected him to. My bulk and attitude gave him pause. He was not only dealing with a wizard, but a guy who could probably pound him into the pavement.

"All right," he said with a sigh. "We work with the basics."

Virgin parchment became white copy paper he took out of the package. The pen and ink was a fountain pen and a cartridge, instead of a quill and inkwell that he sold. I'd find a wand and staff in some woods somewhere. The things we couldn't skimp on were incense, a working knife, and beeswax candles. And I *would* have to buy some new clothes just for this ritual.

We left with two bags full of stuff and D'Luna's cell phone number scrawled on the back of one of his business cards. It would take him an hour, barring traffic, to get down to Rhode Island once I called him.

We got on the highway heading home.

"Bennett," I said. "Mind stopping at a Walmart?"

"For?"

"Need to get special clothes."

"I don't think they sell magic robes at Walmart."

I chuckled. "No, Bennett. Just some clothes that I can dispose of."

"Expecting to get messy?"

I looked out the window. "I hope not."

We got back to Rhode Island around five o'clock, and Bennett took me to a thickly wooded area that technically we weren't allowed to go into, because it was semi-private property. He parked behind a library — an an ancient, ivy-covered, greystone building — and we went into the woods beyond it. The trails were well-established, but I went off the beaten path and followed a deer trail into the woods.

"Do you know where you're going?" Bennett asked, following me.

"I know what I'm looking for," I said. Unfortunately, there was nothing but mighty oaks and maples here. I had hoped for some birch or willow. I stopped at the foot of an oak and dug around in the brush. I found a foot-long piece of wood — and a pair of hooves standing there.

"You know what Ritter will say," said Grimalkin, looking down at me. Bennett was pretty close behind me, so I couldn't say anything. "Ritter will put us back in prison before you can tell him to talk to Pawtucket police.'"

"I know what I'm doing," I said quietly, straightening and holding the stick in my hand. This would be consecrated as a wand. "One down, one to go," I said to Bennett.

"Ritter will destroy us if he does not catch us," Grimalkin said as I walked away from him, pretending he wasn't there. He stayed by my side, his ethereal form passing through trees and branches like a shadow. "He will kill you."

I was fully aware of that possibility. If I stayed with Bennett, I should be safe. And as long as I didn't have the *Key* — D'Luna suggested that he keep the book — Ritter had nothing to pin on me. Bennett was going to hold onto the items we had just bought.

"I got no cell service here," he said, looking at his phone.

"I know," I said, more to answer Grimalkin than to respond to Bennett.

"If he kills you, then I cannot go home," said Grimalkin. "You promised."

I promised to send him back to Hell. He had no power here other than what I could give him, but he had knowledge, and I needed him for that. He knew it, too. He was how I learned most of my spells. Human memory, the memory of other wizards, was spotty and inaccurate. But Grimalkin, a keeper of Grimoires — books of magical spells — was a font of information that I didn't want to send back.

"He won't kill me," I said quietly. "Provided it's just a banishing."

There, in the middle of a field, was a small grove of birch trees. I strode across the field, heading right for them. If I could find a staff, that would be perfect. I left Bennett behind in the dust as I went through the tall grass, my eyes on the prize.

"Watch out," called Grimalkin, and I stopped short. I was about to step into a rabbit hole, and possibly twist my ankle. I carefully went around it, and continued more slowly over to the trees.

Brushing aside bark and leaves, I found a thick branch that was a good six and a half feet tall, at least. It was a little taller and thicker than I would have liked, but I picked it up anyway, brushing the dirt off of it.

"This is fine," I said.

"Good. Let's get out of here," Bennett said.

"Don't like the comforts of nature?" This reminded me of my excursions with Aunt Jane. I looked around the area, breathing in the thick, oxygen-filled air of the trees. "It's beautiful here."

"We're gonna be full of deer ticks."

"Don't be silly."

"I already picked one off my sleeve."

We started walking back through the field, leaving Grimalkin behind. Luckily, I had a good sense of direction, and we found our way back to the car. Bennett insisted on checking me over for ticks — there weren't any — and wanted me to check him over. He didn't have any, either.

Instead of going to Walmart, he brought me to K-Mart. It was the same kind of store, I guess: a department store, but with a lot less to choose from. I picked out a black shirt and black jeans. Hey, since he was paying for it, might as well, right? He also picked up a pizza.

He dropped me off at home just before seven. I had been gone for twelve hours.

"As soon as they call me, I'll let you know," Bennett said. "They've got to find that dog."

I took out D'Luna's business card from the bag. "Maybe Belial's not with the dog. Maybe he returned to the conjurer, like the demons returned to me when they completed their tasks." I tapped the card against my chin. "I'm going to call him."

"What for?"

"To see if he can come down and find where the guy is. He sort of did before, but I cut him off."

"You were an asshole, Mike," said Bennett. "Now get the hell outta my car."

I did, lifting the door as I closed it. "Call me tomorrow," I said.

The next day, I brought my books back to the library and went in the stacks to look for more. Jessica wasn't in to help me with checking out. I walked over to the Mythology section and figured I'd look at whatever else caught my fancy as I walked by.

Tucked in with the mythology books were tomes on religion. I looked around, knowing that if I was among the religion books, I could be among the magic books as well.

Nothing. I knew from experience that magic books didn't last long in a public library. I moved back to the Mythology section. I found a book on Hecate, but thought that might be getting too close to magic, since Hecate was the Greek and Roman goddess of witchcraft. Instead, I took down a large, two-inch thick illustrated encyclopedia of the Egyptian gods. I carried it to the chair that I had taken at the back of the stacks … and found Ritter sitting in it.

"Was wondering how long it was going to take you," said Ritter, making a steeple of his hands and resting his chin on his fingers. "What's that there?"

"Egyptian gods," I said.

"Changing your pantheon?"

"Thinking about it."

He sat back in the chair. "So. Who is the man you keep visiting at the store?"

"None of your business."

"He's a good witch," Ritter mused. "Not someone whose company you would enjoy." Ritter rested back. "Trying to corrupt him?"

"No, for crying out loud!"

"What about the fight outside of the restaurant a few days ago?"

"Do you know what that guy was doing?" I asked.

"Yes," Ritter flatly stated. "He was going to screw a prostitute in the back alley."

"He was going to rape her."

He fell silent for a minute. "So you took it upon yourself to stop it. For what?"

"C'mon, Ritter. Can't you believe that I can actually do some good?"

"It's only for you to get something out of it. That's what people like you do good deeds for — for glory and fame and recognition."

"The girl ran away; she didn't stop and thank me. And I didn't tell Scott so that he would be all impressed with me. Right, Ritter. Why don't you do something that you're trained to do, and find Belial?"

"Do you not think we're already working on it? Once we find him, he will be banished, and we will find who did it, and either destroy him or bring him to prison. Why are you involving yourself in this?"

"Because the Pawtucket police involved me."

"The Pawtucket police are not supposed to involve you."

"I'm cheaper than you guys."

"You're doing this for another reason." Ritter kept worrying on that bone like a starving dog. "Maybe you want Belial for yourself."

"He already tempted me with world domination. I'm not interested in that."

"Of course not," said Ritter with a sneer. "You want to destroy us."

I wanted to admit it aloud, but it wouldn't make Ritter shake in his boots. It would make him arrest me for threatening a Knight Templar in the middle of his duties.

I said, instead, "Do you mind moving out of that chair? I was planning on reading there."

Ritter didn't move. In fact, he stretched out in the chair, making himself comfortable.

I made a disgusted noise. "Come on, Ritter. If I do something, it's not because I want fame, fortune, glory, or power. I do it because the police asked me to."

"What are they asking you to do?"

Well, I decided, *I might as well admit it.* "The Pawtucket cops are asking me to banish Belial."

"And you're going to do it?"

"Once they find him. But I don't know where he is."

"Who told you to do this?"

"Hotchkiss." I thought I saw a flicker behind Ritter's usually empty grey eyes. "You know him?"

"He knows us. I'm surprised he hasn't called us about this." He rose gracefully from the chair. "Maybe it's true, you are cheaper. But then, you get what you pay for."

He walked up to me until we stood eye to eye. He searched my eyes, trying to see beyond them to the soul, to the real reason I was doing this. I suppose he was satisfied, because he took a step back.

"I'll check with him. In the meantime, don't screw this up."

"You're giving me permission?" My heart leapt again. I was being allowed to use magic!

"I'm telling you not to screw this up. This is *Belial*. He won't go down easy." He strode by me. "Oh, and don't expect any help from me."

"Wasn't planning on it," I said.

Ritter kept on going, then dipped down one of the aisles. I went to the chair. I could smell his scent in the air for a moment — of thick, wet wood.

"Hello?" said D'Luna.

"Hey."

"Did they find him?"

"No. That's what I'm calling you about." I was walking home, carrying four books in a tote bag that the library let me have for free. "You said you can see spirits."

"Yes ..."

"Can you sense them? Like where they are?"

"I see where you're going with this, Mike. Can I call you Mike?"

"Sure."

"Then you can call me Sebastian. I see what you're saying. I can be there in an hour, if you want to try to find him. I'll meet you at the place where the sigil was found."

"If I can get a ride there. If I can't, can I meet you somewhere else?" I stopped walking, turned around, and headed back. I could kill some time at the Y while waiting for him.

"Yes," D'Luna replied. "I'll call you once I get to Rhode Island."

At the Y, I put my books in a locker and did a light workout, since I didn't have my gym clothes with me. I meditated in the empty TV room, trying to calm my mind. It was racing, wondering what would happen if we found the conjurer, if we could find Belial, how to banish him, and what to do afterwards. I was thinking of "we". This is the first time I thought of having another person with me to do the work, and I wasn't sure what to have him do.

I finally calmed down enough, but by then, my phone rang.

"I'm in Rhode Island," said D'Luna. "Where are you?"

"At the Pawtucket Library," I said, getting up from the chair I meditated in. "I'll be on the front steps."

I gathered my books and went to the front steps. I heard two beeps, and turned to see a Honda Accord parked right in front of the library. I went over to the car, and D'Luna leaned over the seat.

"Mike."

"Hi." I got in, habitually lifting the door when closing it. I looked around at the car's interior. "Nice car."

"I'm still paying for it," he said. He didn't seem to be that much of a dick anymore, now that we were working together. Maybe Bennett was right, I considered, and I was the dick.

He pulled out into traffic and we drove toward Slater Park.

"What do you think you'll find?" he asked.

"At least the conjurer," I said. "If we can find him, then we can possibly find Belial." If he didn't jump from the dog to a human.

"How it worked for you isn't the way things normally work," said D'Luna. "You must have given your demon a lot of power to have him influence the world without having a vessel."

I didn't want to talk about it anymore. Maybe Belial and Andromalius were unique. Or maybe I was. I just fell silent as we drove.

When we got to the spot where the demon was summoned, D'Luna took out a thick, silver pendulum. He popped the top of it — it was a silver triangular locket, so he could put something in it. He gathered up a little bit of dirt from the edge of the area and put it in the pendulum. Then he let it swing.

It pointed south. He took it with him to the car, and hung it from the rear-view mirror. "I want one of those," I said.

"Seventeen ninety-nine plus tax," he said, and started the car. We followed the pendulum directly south, heading into Providence, and then through the city.

"Long way for this guy to go," I said, as D'Luna got off the highway in an area called Cranston.

"He might have grown up in Pawtucket," offered D'Luna. The pendulum swung sideways and, at this point, I didn't know where it was pointing. "We're close."

I couldn't tell, but he turned left, and we ended up going down a four-lane street. He took another left as we went by a Garden City mall, and then made a right at the end of the street.

"Do you really have any idea where you're going?" I asked.

He glared at me when we reached a stoplight. "You're the one who called me. Remember?"

I was soon lost. Now, he drove very slowly down a residential street. He peered out the window, looking around, only glancing at the pendulum that swung straight in a very fast sawing motion.

"Close, very close ..."

He pulled to a stop in front of a white single-level house. Large and spread out, it filled the plot of land from end to end. The lawn in front of it had strategically-placed assorted lawn decorations. No cars were parked in its driveway, although the garage was big enough for one car.

D'Luna parked the car. "He's in here," he said.

"Are you sure?"

The pendulum was swinging wildly toward me, toward the house. It swung so hard that it almost struck the inside of the windshield.

He grabbed the pendulum and kept it still for a moment. When he let it go, it started swinging again toward the house.

"What do you think?" he asked me, and got out of the car.

"Wait!" I called to him.

I got out on my side. I wondered what we were going to be meeting up against. Would it be a man possessed by a legion of devils? Or a woman with kids tugging at her pants? The lawn had a woman's touch, which meant to me that there was a woman in there somewhere.

D'Luna came around the front of the car to my side. "I usually have the cops with me when I go in," he said. "Lord knows what we'll be facing. Do you have defensive spells?"

"Personal defense," I said.

"Then every man for himself," he said, and crossed the lawn.

I followed him. The lawn was thick and cushiony underfoot, although it needed to be cut. We passed a pair of pink flamingos and a litter of garden gnomes before we got to the tiled walkway. At the door, D'Luna glanced around the doorframe, looking, I suspected, for any kind of wards or booby traps. I didn't spot any, myself.

He rang the doorbell. A dog yipped inside. We watched as the door opened and an old woman, stooped over and leaning on a walker, cracked open the door.

"Yes?" she asked, her voice sounding husky and raspy, like she'd had too many cigarettes. The smell that wafted from inside the house was old, moldy.

"Hello," said D'Luna with a smile, turning on obvious charm. "We're assisting the Pawtucket Police. Is your son or husband home?"

Both of us could tell that this woman was not the person who had done the actual sigil, but whoever it was had been living in this house.

"Who's that, gramma?" called a boy's voice, while the dog barked again.

The boy came to the door, pulling it open a little wider. He was a heavy-set kid, about twelve or thirteen. I could see the family resemblance in the shape of his face and the set of his eyes. While gramma's eyes were rheumy blue and wet, the boy's eyes were clear dark blue.

"They're from the police, dear," she said, and waved her hand, trying to push him further back into the house.

"I didn't do anything," the boy said immediately.

Now, I got into demon summoning at the age of eleven, so it wouldn't surprise me if this was the person we wanted. D'Luna, though, didn't think so.

"We're not looking for you. We're looking for your father."

D'Luna didn't bring up the husband. The husband, even if he was younger, had to be at least thirty years older than me, and might not have the stamina to get from the car to the trees at the park.

"He's at work," said gramma.

"Why are you saying you didn't do anything?" I asked the boy.

The boy backed away.

Gramma glared at me. "Does this have to do with those boys at school?"

"What boys at school?" I asked.

"Mike."

D'Luna nodded his head toward the lawn. I glowered, but I stepped off the small entranceway onto the walkway.

"Excuse my friend," said D'Luna with a smile to the old woman. "What time will he be getting off work?"

"Five," said gramma. That was about an hour from now.

"Where does he work?"

"Amica. He works in the office."

D'Luna nodded. "We'll wait here, if you don't mind. I didn't catch his name …"

"Marty DePasquale."

"Right. Thank you." D'Luna stepped down from the entranceway. "We'll be right outside here." We walked back to his car.

"Are you sure about this?" I asked him as we walked back to the car. "What if they call the cops?"

"They think we *are* the cops," he told me. "Have you ever done this before?"

"No."

"This is how the cops handle it."

Marty pulled in the driveway just before six. D'Luna and I were standing outside of D'Luna's car, trying to look casual. Marty hauled himself from his car. Like the kid, he was also heavy. He wore a light-colored, button-down shirt. He looked exactly like I had pictured the man from the park: chiseled features, brown hair, clean-shaven, but thick, horn-rimmed glasses covered his eyes. Panting, he looked over toward us.

"Mr. DePasquale," D'Luna called to him. "Can we have a word with you?"

D'Luna strode across the lawn, as if he had a purpose. I just shut up and followed like a dutiful puppy. We had discussed that he was going to take the lead; I'd grudgingly accepted. When we got closer to DePasquale, I could smell him: sweat and rusted iron and magic.

I assumed that D'Luna could see the magic as well, because he was looking over at DePasquale as if he had three heads.

"Mr. DePasquale," said D'Luna, "Were you in Slater Park about two weeks ago?"

"I don't know what you're talking about," he said, and started toward the door of the house.

D'Luna put a hand out. I stepped in DePasquale's way.

"If you don't leave these premises, I will call the police," DePasquale said. He tried to sound tough. In his nervousness, it came out breathless.

"You did a summoning," I said.

DePasquale forced a laugh. I could tell it was forced, because he put his hands on his hips, threw back his head, and brayed.

"What are you talking about?"

"You summoned a demon."

DePasquale put a hand on my chest, right above my heart. I felt the power now. It was like fire and electricity at the same time, and it was going to course through me in a shock. I put my hand on his forearm and tightened my grip on him.

"You're supposed to fall down," he said, slowly growing confused. "Why don't you fall down?"

I kept my grip tight on his arm, blocking the flow of energy to his hand. I stepped out from under his touch and pushed his hand sideways away from me.

"I'm a wizard," I said. "We both are."

"Did you do the summoning?" D'Luna asked him again.

"What's it to you?" he demanded of D'Luna. "I have the power to stop people, to remove people in my way, and you know what? I'll be Vice President in this division once I get all the people out of the way." He looked up at the house. "And then I won't have to bring my son to this bitch's house any more." He glared at me now. "Let me go inside, or I'll do something really bad."

"You got the power in exchange for what?" I said.

He shrugged. "What's it to you? You going to let me go? Or do I have to get rough with you?"

As he spoke, I watched his eyes. They were turning from deep blue to a cold, translucent and glowing blue, It filled his entire eye, white and all.

I raised my left hand to my chest and made a sign of protection, while I pushed him away with my right hand that was around his forearm. His skin had grown cold to the touch — ice cold.

He roared. It was a like a real roar, not a sound that a man would make. He threw his head back and when he opened his eyes to look at me, his eyes were filled with a blue fire.

He opened his mouth, exhaling snow and ice at me.

I bent my head and closed my eyes, but kept my hand raised in that protective sign, as ice covered the pink flamingoes with white frost. Then it stopped, and I opened my eyes to see D'Luna and Marty rolling among the garden gnomes and the rocks next to the walkway.

Marty punched D'Luna in the face so hard that he fell over and off of him. I ran at Marty as he started to get up, tackling him. I saw how he hit D'Luna, so I tried the same move. He blocked my punch with one hand, and I felt him pour the snow over his hand and onto my own, attempting to freeze my hand.

I kneed him in the groin. I know, it was a dirty move, but it was the only thing I could think of.

He doubled over in pain, his hand letting go of mine. D'Luna got up, bleeding from his nose. He grabbed Marty by the scruff of his neck and yanked him up. He yelled at me.

"Banish it!"

I hastily made the sign of the cross the best I could with my half-frozen right hand.

"Belial, I command you, go in peace, with no harm to man or beast —"

"Ha!" Marty yelled. "I'm not Belial, you idiot!"

He turned and slapped at D'Luna, who dropped Marty to get out of the way of the man's swinging hand.

"Tell me your name," I demanded. "I command it in the name of the Lord."

Marty was on his own two feet now, and I could hear the sirens. His shirt was ripped, his face pale, almost blue. His glasses were gone, but he was staring right at me and could probably see me just fine.

"You mouth the words, but you have no faith."

He was right; I had no faith. So I rushed him again, shoving him halfway across the lawn before wrestling him back to the ground again, cracking his head hard against the cement blocks that lined the walkway. I held him down by his arms.

"Tell me your name!"

Marty — or the creature that possessed him — laughed and I felt him building power. He was going to hit me — and hit me hard — with frost, and I had no way to protect myself. I sat up, losing my leverage, and then I felt someone grab me by my arms and yank me off him, dragging me away. Two police officers dragged me back a few yards and dumped me onto the lawn.

Marty rose. He was grinning, his eyes still glowing. "That's right," he said. "He attacked me."

The cops looked from Marty to me. One of them had a hand on his gun.

"Marty," called D'Luna called out. "Marty, you can stop this. Marty, if you can hear me —"

Again a roar, and again he vomited snow and ice onto D'Luna. Like me, it went around him, but caught on the car and the lawn, freezing it. Both cops drew their revolvers and aimed them at Marty.

"Don't!" I yelled.

If they destroyed the vessel, the demon would only go to the nearest body and reside there until it had used up that vessel as well.

I jumped up and ran at Marty, again throwing him down on the ground, even while the cops yelled at me to get off of him. If I didn't have his name, I would have to use something different.

"Demon of Hell, I command thee," I yelled as I pulled all my will up my arms and into my hands that were on his shoulders, holding him down. "I command thee to return unto Hell, harming none. Begone, demon of Hell!"

I repeated it the required seven times, even as Marty grabbed at my neck and tried to choke me. But I didn't let go and I didn't stop.

Marty shuddered as I gasped the last utterance and he looked back at me with clear blue eyes. The demon had gone.

I sat back, letting go of Marty's shoulders. I felt dizzy, and felt myself fall sideways off his body, landing onto the lawn to stretch out at the man's side. My breathing was slow and labored, and I knew I was going to pass out.

CHAPTER TWELVE

BELIAL

MY PHONE WAS RINGING. I pawed at my pants, but my arms didn't want to move yet. There was something up my nose. I opened my eyes to see the inside of an ambulance. It was moving.

"You okay?" asked someone sitting next to me. He got up and checked something. There was an IV inserted into the back of my hand, and it hurt like Hell. I was strapped down onto a gurney.

"Yeah," I said. "What happened?"

"Someone tried to choke you and you passed out. You sure you're okay?"

"Yeah."

"What's your name?"

"Mike LeBonte."

"Where do you live?"

"173 Hope Street, Pawtucket. Second floor."

"Do you know what day it is?"

"It was Tuesday last I checked." I paused, trying to focus. "Is my phone ringing?"

"Might be the sirens. We're bringing you to Rhode Island Hospital."

"I'm fine, really. You can drop me off wherever."

He chuckled. "We're not a taxi service."

He was cute, with short black hair, and a pinched face. A little too thin for my taste, but beggars couldn't be choosers, I suppose.

However, one of my own personal fantasies would not be fulfilled at that moment, because we soon pulled into Rhode Island Hospital. I was hefted out of the ambulance, wheeled down a corridor, and whisked into a room. They hoisted me into a bed, leaving me there.

A dark-skinned woman came in after what seemed a long time later. "Hi, Mr. LeBonte," she greeted me with a nod. "I'm Tasha, and I'll be your nurse. Can you tell me what happened?"

"Well, I banished a demon, and I guess I pushed too hard."

She forced a smile. "All right then," she said. "I'll be right back."

She checked my IV, checked the tube that was in my nose, and then left, closing the curtain after her.

I chuckled to myself. The truth would be difficult for them to take, so I guess I had to come up with something else. They were probably already calling the nearest asylum.

Oh, I was definitely going to get out. I patted my pocket and felt my phone there. I looked around the room, didn't see a sign against cell phone use. Unfortunately, it was in the same side pocket as the hand that had my IV, so I had a hard time moving my other hand into that pocket.

The curtain parted and a man came in. "Hello," he said. Tasha trailed behind him. "I'm Dr. Michaels. What seems to have happened?"

"I banished a demon, and I used my will to do it, and I pushed too hard."

"What do you mean, 'pushed too hard'?"

"I used all of my will and I collapsed."

"Are you a priest?"

"A wizard."

"I see." The doctor surprised me. He examined my IV line and was being very clinical. "And you do this often?"

"A couple of times." I tilted my head. "Are you humoring me?"

"No, I believe you." I wasn't sure if he did or not. He was checking my eyes and my vitals as he spoke to me. "This demon," he said. "Where did you banish it to?"

"Back to Hell."

"I see." He stood back. "We are, of course, going to have to check your story."

"Sure. There were cops there."

"I know," Dr. Michaels stated, finally focusing on me. "They're here, too. They want to speak to you when you're feeling better."

"I feel fine," I said, irritated. "In fact, I can go home, right?"

"I don't think you can go home just yet. We want to monitor you for a couple of hours, to make sure you're okay."

I sat back, my head against the pillow. "Fine. I can talk to the police."

The two cops came in a short time after the doctor left. One had a name tag of Alvarez on his uniform. "You okay?" he asked.

"Yeah. I exerted too much. I'll be fine."

"He *was* choking you," said the other cop. His name tag read Gibson.

"Is he okay?" I asked.

"He was a little out of it when we last saw him."

"He's on his way here, as a matter of fact," Alvarez said. "We're going to check on him after talking to you."

"So what started this whole thing?" Gibson asked.

I told them about the summoning in Slater Park, how D'Luna was able to find out who it was, and then who attacked whom first. The cops had seen Marty vomiting snow and ice, knowing that wasn't natural. I must have bumped Marty's head, so maybe that's why he was out of it. I didn't tell them that Belial was running around, though. What they had seen was crazy enough.

Tasha came to the door, "There's a man out here for you, Mr. LeBonte."

"Call me Mike. As soon as these gentlemen are done with me …"

"We're all set," Alvarez said, closing his notepad. "We'll call you if we need anything else."

The cops left, and Tasha escorted D'Luna into my area. He carried the tote bag with my books. "Oh, man, thank you," I said, reaching for the bag.

"Not happy to see me?"

"Happy to see you, too," I said.

"Right. Look, I have to go. Is there anyone you want me to get a hold of for you?"

"I got my phone."

"You're not allowed to use phones in the ER."

"Dammit," I snapped. "All right, I'll ask them to call Dom and Evie."

"We still need to find Belial," he said. "That was a minor demon that you banished. It was too easy."

"I know." I pulled out one of the books, a novel about the Aztecs. It was a door-stopper; huge, but was probably going to be interesting. "I'll work on finding Belial."

"Banishing him is not going to be as easy. You were lucky, Mike. Very lucky."

After he left, I thought about what he said, and realized that yes, I was damn lucky.

I know the hospital wasn't happy with me, because when I told Tasha that I was ready to leave, and if she could contact Dom or Evie, they gave me a phone and I had to call them myself. I tried Dom first. He picked up on the second ring.

"Hey, man, I'm at Rhode Island Hospital and —"

"What're you doing there?"

"The ambulance brought me here."

"Why did you go for a ride in an ambulance?"

"It's a long story, Dom. Can you come and get me? They won't let me go unless I have a ride."

"Oh, Mike. I'm up in Woonsocket covering a game."

That was a good half-hour or more away, depending on traffic. "Okay, um, let me try and get someone else." I had Bennett's number. Hopefully, he wasn't at the casino.

After I hung up with Dom, I called Bennett.

"Yello."

"Bennett, it's Mike. I'm in the hospital."

"No wonder. I tried to call you earlier, but you didn't answer."

"You did?"

"Yeah. They found the dog. They think it's rabid, but they're keeping it alive for you."

"Gee, isn't that nice of them."

"You think you can come down tonight and do that ritual?"

"Tonight?"

"They'll rope off Slater Park for you to do that ritual in the same place that the other guy did it."

"I need a ride," I said, "D'Luna's on his way home — dammit, I didn't memorize his cell phone."

"Didn't you program it into your phone?"

"No, I don't know how to do that."

"Shit. You're going to have to do that ritual yourself, then. You think you can?"

"You have all the stuff." I didn't have the *Key of Solomon*, so I was going to have to wing it.

"Yeah, I know. Is that all you need? Don't you need an acolyte or something?"

"No, I don't need one. It's nice to have one, but I can do this myself." I did it before, right?

"I'll come get you out of the hospital," Bennett said.

"Okay."

I hung up, and sat back, waiting for Tasha to come back.

And waited.

I called Dom, but he didn't answer, so I left him a voicemail saying I got a ride and was going to be late.

At ten o'clock, about five hours after I got into the ER, Bennett arrived. "They haven't disconnected you yet."

"I know." I raised my left hand, the one with the IV in it. "Tasha hasn't been in for about an hour."

"You could always pull it out and walk out yourself."

I shivered. I hate needles.

Bennett threw open the curtain. "Hey, we're ready to leave."

"Be with you in a moment," someone replied.

"Pawtucket Police wants him. Right. Now."

Finally, just before 11 o'clock, we were on the highway back to Pawtucket. I cradled my left hand gingerly. "This is the hand I need to do the ritual with."

"Is that bad?"

"I don't know." I had a bandage over the wound the IV's needle had caused — the needle had been huge and I had almost passed out when I watched the nurse pull it out. I didn't want to look at my hand; even just thinking about the needle gave me the willies. "I shouldn't let any blood leak."

We pulled into Slater Park. Three police cars and an Animal Control van were parked in the lot. Lanterns lit up the area where the ritual would happen. I got out of the car, grabbing the bags of stuff that Bennett had bought.

Hotchkiss and five cops stood in the illuminated area. They had trampled down the grass, leaving it flat. The dog lay down in the grass — tranquilized, I assumed.

"You sure you know what you're doing?" Hotchkiss asked, watching me unpack.

"I've done this before," I told him. "I think, though, that I should do this by myself." I glanced at the cops. "I don't want anyone getting hurt."

"I'm staying," said Hotchkiss.

"Do you have a crucifix?"

He unfastened the top button of his shirt, loosened his tie, and pulled out a small gold crucifix on a thin chain. "I was my mother's," he said. "Good Irish Catholic."

I looked at the other cops. They looked like they didn't want to be there.

"Okay, then," I said to Hotchkiss. "But you have to stay out of my way."

As the cops went back to the cars, I started to draw the circle with salt. I had two pounds of salt: one pound for the demon, the other pound for me. I poured the salt in a general circle around the dog, creating the demon's containment circle first. I then created my own, making it a little bigger to accommodate Hotchkiss. As I poured the salt, I pushed my will for protection into the circle.

Next, I set a fire in a small cauldron, using some dry sticks I found. I kept the cauldron with me, in my protective circle. I also started the incense burner, which was a small piece of coal with saltpeter threaded through it, so that it could stay smoldering. I had a cup, but no water.

"Do you have any water?"

"Maybe the guys do," said Hotchkiss. "Can I leave?"

"I haven't started the conjuring yet. You can leave."

I took out a large pentacle tile about the size of my outstretched hand and set it down on the ground. With a charcoal stick, I drew Belial's sigil on the back. I was not about to use my blood because I didn't want to tie him to me. Ritter wouldn't care much for that. Neither would I.

Hotchkiss returned with a bottle of water. "Here."

"Is it fresh?"

"Yeah."

I heard it click open as I unscrewed the cap. After pouring the water into the cup, I walked over to the conjuring circle. I sprinkled some water in the circle.

"By the element of Water, I consecrate this circle."

Next, I got the cauldron. I held it up over the circle.

"By the element of Fire, I consecrate this circle."

I got the censer — an old fashioned one with a chain and everything. I shook it over the conjuring circle.

"By the element of Air, I consecrate this circle."

Last, I stomped on the ground.

"By the element of Earth, I consecrate this circle."

I returned to my protective circle and summoned the elements to protect us.

As I sprinkled the water over both of us, I said, "By the element of Water, Guardian of the West, protect us."

I did the same thing with Fire and Air, handing Hotchkiss some of the dirt from the ground we stood on for the element of Earth.

I walked around the circle, pointing the wand down toward the ground. The dog whimpered in its sleep. I walked from west, to south, to east, to north. *Widdershins,* it's known as, counter-clockwise.

I could sense the protective circle around us. It was tight, as Hotchkiss was a slightly big guy. He stepped back to the edge, and I noticed that he jumped when he got to the edge of the circle. He didn't say anything, but I saw him put his hands in his pockets and then shiver.

I raised my arms above my head and cried out, "Behold us, prepared to conjure ye, Belial, by the names and symbols of God, wherewith we are fortified, and by the virtue of the highest one. We command ye, Belial, and potently ordain ye by the most strong and powerful name of God, EL, who is worthy of all praise, admiration, honor, glory, admiration, and fear. Ye shall delay not longer, but that ye, Belial, appear before us without any tumult or disturbance, but, on the contrary, with great respect and courtesy, in a beautiful human form."

The woods remained silent.

I had expected this. I studied the conjuring circle, making sure I had done it correctly. The dog whimpered again. I repeated the conjuration again, louder this time, pushing more of my will into it.

Then I said it again.

The dog barked once. Its whole body went rigid, as if it was having a seizure. Then it stiffly got to its feet, a puppet on strings. It exhaled sickly green fog, then collapsed.

The fog roiled, and then resolved itself into a man clad in full armor. A helmet covered his face, but his eyes were white orbs. I didn't ask Hotchkiss what he saw, as I was concentrating on the conjuration.

I showed the pentacle to the man in armor. "Obey ye, Belial. Obey ye, Belial. Obey ye, Belial, behold the symbols and names of the creator. Be gentle and peaceable and obey all things that we shall command ye."

"Boy wizard," Belial said, his voice almost a growl. "Ye summon me for what purpose?"

"I summon ye to send ye home."

Belial lifted his hand from his sword hilt, and crossed his huge arms, clad in armor only up to his elbows. "Ye are not a Knight. Why do their work?"

I had no answer. I held my hands up at my chest, my palms outward. "I command ye to return to Hell."

He laughed like I had told him a funny joke.

I kind of figured he'd do that. So I began the banishment evocation and pushed my will into it:

"In the name of ADONAI, the eternal and everlasting one, let ye return unto his place; be there peace between us and you." I then began to quote the first chapter of Genesis. "In the beginning, God created Heaven and earth ..."

He only smiled while I started the recitation. This was when he should start railing, telling me lies, telling me that I couldn't send him back, that I didn't have the power or the will. This was when he'd throw himself against the edge of the circle's barrier, testing my abilities. This was when he'd scream in agony and fury, cursing me, saying that he would claim my soul.

At least that's what Andromalius had done. But Belial didn't do that.

He merely faded away while I spoke. By the time I got to the end of the first chapter of Genesis, he was gone.

I was confused, but I didn't dare show it to Hotchkiss.

I glanced back at him. "You okay?"

"Yeah." He stared down at the circle we were in. "Is that it?"

"Did you see anything?"

"I saw someone in armor. I think. It was kind of shadowy."

I used the athame to cut the circle open, feeling the chill air around us now. I poured the water over the fire in the cauldron and the censer, putting those fires out.

"That's it," I said, though something nagged at me.

Belial hadn't fought me. Usually demons liked to stay in this world; it was more exciting and offered some diversions to the eternity of Hell.

I stepped out of the circle.

"You can come out now," I told Hotchkiss.

He took a few tentative steps. "So it's all over?"

"Yeah," I said, trying to sound confident.

I should have felt elated. I didn't. I felt confused. Why didn't Belial fight going back to Hell? Did he leave behind a booby trap of some sort?

The dog wasn't moving. Hotchkiss walked up to the animal and gently nudged it with his foot.

"He's dead."

I looked down, and offered a prayer to the poor dog's soul.

CHAPTER THIRTEEN

TWO DATES

EVIE WAS UP WAITING FOR ME when the police car dropped me off. I'm sure that looked good to the landlady — if she was still looking out her window at two in the morning.

"Is everything okay?" she asked, when I walked in the door. Rufus greeted me with a head-butt and a slow wag of his tail. He looked just as tired as Evie did.

"Yeah. You didn't have to wait up for me."

"I wanted to be sure you were all right," Evie said. Her eyelids were heavy.

"Go to sleep, Evie," I said to her. "I'm fine."

Evie gave me a kiss on the cheek and went to her bedroom, shutting the door behind her. I undressed in the dark.

"Grimalkin," I called quietly. "I summon thee."

He appeared in a flash, standing in front of the entertainment center like he had the first night I was free.

"You think you did not succeed," he said.

"Something's wrong." I admitted. "Belial didn't fight me."

"It is possible he wanted to return," said Grimalkin. "I know some spirits like that."

"Very funny," I snapped, kicking my pants up so I could grab them from the air, instead of having to bend down for them. I folded them absently, saying, "I did the spell correctly, right?"

"You took shortcuts," Grimalkin said, sounding like he was tired. "Your will was strong enough."

I put my will into the circles, into the invocation and the evocation. I might have gotten some of the Book of Genesis wrong, but the words aren't what drives the demon; it's the magician's will. I had thrown out the spirit in Marty's vessel. I knew I forced Belial to Hell.

"You succeeded," Grimalkin stated, as if he was just saying this to get me to dismiss him. I wasn't going to let him go that easy. I needed this debriefing. "Belial might have claimed souls and wanted to return to Hell to torture them for eternity."

Belial could have claimed the soul of the policeman he possessed. Or the man in the school. Or even the dog.

"All right," I said, feeling a little better. "Is that why you want to return to Hell?"

"If I claimed souls," said Grimalkin. "It would have been yours."

"After all I've done for you," I said with a smirk.

He snorted. "Not quite."

At that, he walked through the entertainment center and disappeared.

The next morning, I begged for some money from Dom and Evie. "I want to take this guy out on a date," I said.

Evie handed me fifty dollars. Dom raised an eyebrow at that.

"It's a first date," she explained to Dom. "Besides, do you want Mikey to be living with us after we're married?"

Dom must have thought that would be a terrible idea, so he shut up.

He and Evie went out for the morning, and I left about a few hours later, walking to downtown. It was a fine day, not too warm and not too cold. I couldn't believe that it was almost mid-May. Flowers were in bloom in people's front yards, birds were singing, and I was a free man.

I got to the White Raven a little after 11:30, but the place was still closed. Maybe he wasn't up early, I thought, so I hung around for a little while. Around noon, I saw him walking up the street from the parking garage.

He saw me and smiled, crossing the street. "Sorry I'm late," he said. "I didn't want to get out of bed this morning."

"That's all right."

He smelled of woods, a fresh shower. He opened the door, turned off the alarm, and went to the back room. "So what's up?"

"I banished that demon," I told him.

He stopped what he was doing. "You did? When?"

"Last night. The Pawtucket cops were there and everything."

"That's great! You should celebrate."

"I am. I want to take you out to dinner tonight."

He blushed. Damn, he looked so cute when he blushed.

"Thing is, you'll have to drive us there."

"Can't you fly?" He said it with a wink, so I couldn't get mad at him.

"Yes, but you can't."

He laughed. "Do you like Chinese buffets?"

"As long as they don't have wieners."

"They don't. I haven't been to one in a while, and since you're paying …"

"Oh, I get it."

He tilted his head to the side, thrust out his lower lip, and looked up at me from lidded eyes. I chuckled.

"All right, we can go there."

"Yay!" he said with a coy grin. "My begging look worked."

I wanted to put my arm around his shoulders and give him a kiss. I looked at him across the counter, with all those thoughts and more swirling around in my head. What if he could sense what I was thinking, that I wanted more than a first date, that I could imagine the two of us, together somewhere — some place where it was safe for the two of us to walk hand in hand, watch the sunset or the moonrise as we sat on a grassy hill, him in my arms, leaning against me …

Man, I was looking way too far ahead. Prison had made me a romantic, it seemed. In there, it was all about sex and power: who was stronger, who was on top, who could make the other person do what they wanted. I didn't want to have that kind of relationship with Scott. I wanted to give him flowers and dinner, a movie and some cuddling.

I looked down and away, my eye caught by the fake wands in the case. "Are those new?"

"No," he said, looking at where my eyes had gone. "Those are for the *Harry Potter* types."

"Ah," I said. Glancing up at him again, he had a confused look on his face. "I'm, ah, gonna go to the library and the gym, if that's okay?"

"Sure."

"I'll be back around four."

"Okay," he said with a smile. "I'll close up early."

I retreated to the door and put my hand on it. Why was I running away? I didn't bring my gym clothes, and I sure didn't need to go to the library. But I was sure running away. I was running away from the emotions this brought up in me. I left him there, probably feeling confused.

Maybe I could work it out, I decided. I walked back home, grabbed my gym bag, and walked all the way back to the gym.

I soaked in the pool after my workout, my mind finally slowing down enough for me to think about what I was going to do. *Should I get him flowers? A little present? What kind of things does he like?* Up the road a little bit was a Spanish supermarket which might have some trinkets. I shook my head to myself. *No, I wouldn't be able to afford that and dinner … flowers maybe.*

As I debated these things, I saw the man who had accosted the little boy a couple of days ago. He was trim, with a runner's body. I could take him down easily.

The man dove into the pool and started swimming toward me. I had two options: stand my ground, and probably drown the guy if he was going to come after me, or leave. I chose the latter.

I headed back inside the locker room to the showers. It was around 2:30, which meant I had plenty of time to kill before my date with Scott at four o'clock. I ducked my head under the shower head to rinse out the chlorine. A moment later, I felt something cold and wet against my butt.

I whirled around, my arms out, and whacked across at whoever was there. It was a move I had learned in prison. I knocked the person to the floor. Blinking the water from my eyes, I saw the man from the pool lay sprawled on the floor. I hadn't broken anything, unfortunately.

He wore blue Speedos, but they were not hiding a firm erection that peeked out from beneath the waistband of his tight shorts. He was shocked, stunned, and then became angry.

"What the Hell, man?" he yelled at me, putting his hands on the slick tile and trying to rise.

I only glared at him. Even though I tried, I couldn't come up with anything more clever than, *"You sick bastard."*

He got to his feet. "From the way you were looking at me," he said. "I thought you wanted it."

"No," I said. "I wanted to kill you."

"Kill me?" He tried to turn on charm. It wasn't going to work. "Why?"

"You were going to pull that little boy in here and molest him. Just like you were going to do to me."

He blushed and chuckled lowly. "What makes you think that?"

"Because I know people like you. I *lived* with people like you. And I'll be damned if I let you get away with anything like that."

"Man, you are messed up in the head," he said. He moved in close to me.

I grabbed his bits. He yelped, and I quickly uttered a spell. No more erections over little boys. No more erections. Ever. Period.

I released him, and he stumbled back. He stared at me like I was the one molesting him, and bolted from the showers.

I washed my hands of it. Literally.

I arrived at The White Raven with a bouquet of flowers. Well, there were exactly four flowers and a whole lot of greens. The Spanish market had been selling them.

Scott smiled when I came in with the flowers. "Those are so nice! Thank you! Let me get a vase."

He slipped into the back room and came back with a long vase. The flowers were a little too long for it, so he cut them before putting them inside it. When he finished arranging them, they looked a lot fuller than they had in the bouquet I bought. He stepped back and admired his handiwork, and smiled at me.

"So," I asked. "Where is this buffet?"

"East Providence," he replied. "Not too far." He started toward the door, dangling keys. I stepped outside while he shut off most of the lights, turned the sign to "Closed", set the alarm, and then locked up. "Follow me," he said.

His car turned out to be a small truck, something I hadn't expected him to drive, an older-model blue Ford Ranger. It sported a little bit of body rot around the passenger side rear tire well, otherwise it seemed in good condition. He moved some stuff that was on the front seat to behind it, and then patted the seat cushion.

"Okay, get in."

I did, laying my gym bag on the floor. I noticed the truck was a stick-shift. Most of the vehicles I had seen thus far were automatics. I hadn't seen a manual since before I went to prison.

"This isn't what I expected," I said, as he climbed into the driver's seat.

"What did you expect?"

"Something fancy. A BMW?"

"Can't move a lot of inventory in a BMW," he said with a chuckle. "Besides, the deal for this one was too good to pass up." He backed out of the spot and deftly sped through the parking garage.

I listened to the radio. It was mostly ambient noise and an obnoxious DJ, with hardly any music. "Is this place any good?"

"I like it. I used to go here a lot."

"By yourself?"

"No. An ex."

"You broke up?"

"This was a while ago. When I first moved here."

"Why did you break up?"

He shrugged. "It just didn't work out. He wanted me to introduce him to my family."

"I could introduce you to mine," I said.

"They know?"

"Well, my sister and soon-to-be brother-in-law. I suspect my parents know, but they don't know I'm back."

"You still didn't tell them?"

I shook my head. "I want them to know on my terms. I was thinking maybe the wedding."

"Mike, I know I'm estranged from my family, so I shouldn't talk. But at least tell your mom. She probably wants to see you."

"She doesn't know I was in prison," I said as he took a left into a strip mall's parking lot. "I'm not sure I want them to know. They wouldn't understand."

"You should tell them the truth."

He drove to the far end of the strip mall, to a corner where it said in big red letters above a wall of glass, *East Buffet*. He parked at the side of the building.

"'Tell the truth, but tell it slant,'" I said, getting out of the truck. I heard him laugh.

We walked to the front of the building. He let me into the foyer, and I held the door open for him to the restaurant proper. It was huge, with a long set of buffet tables at the end of the room, surrounded in a U-shape by tables and chairs and booths. We picked a booth, and sat across from each other. The young girl took our order and motioned for us to hit the buffet.

I took a plate, and was overwhelmed with the scents and sights of all of the food. I took a little bit of everything on the first table.

When I got back to our booth, Scott had piled his plate high with sushi. "This is the only place that does sushi," he said. "For $12.95, it's worth it."

"When I get the money from Pawtucket," I said, "I'll treat you to a real Japanese restaurant."

"Don't be crazy. This is good." He popped one in his mouth and made a sound of satisfaction. "Want one?"

"I didn't see them," I said, and plucked one from his plate.

"The best stuff is in the middle," he said. "Sometimes at the end of that middle table, they put out some real Chinese food. Like prawns and stuff." He shrugged. "But most times, it's crab legs. People stand in line, waiting for them, and then pounce on them when they show up."

"What's the big deal about that?"

"It's crab meat. Expensive and worth your money."

I took a few nibbles of my food. I was careful not to take too much, because I didn't want to end up sick again.

"You said you were estranged."

"Yeah. They wanted me to go to West Point, or be in the military, and instead I opened a magic store." He chuckled. "Man, was dad pissed. Mom was pissed too. We're only civil to each other."

"See, now, that's what I'm afraid of."

"Your sister, did she not talk to you?"

"Well, no. She picked me up at the station the day I got out."

"Then your mom should be like that. Apples don't fall far from the tree."

"I don't know." I pushed around my food. "My sister knew about it." I waved a hand. "She accepted it."

"Anyone else in your family know?"

"My brother found out, but he died."

"Oh," he said, looking down and not eating. "Oh, I'm sorry."

I shook my head. "Don't be. He's not worth being sorry over."

I could still see him in my mind's eye, running across the lawn toward me, screaming, "You faggot!", and then dropping dead right in the middle of the lawn, landing face down in the grass, his arms flung out from his body, like he was trying to fly and the ground had risen up to meet him.

"You didn't have a good relationship."

"Not at all."

"I'm sorry about that, then."

We ate in silence — or relative silence — talking mostly about the food, and how he liked true Chinese food, not this Americanized stuff that passed for Chinese. He was smart, funny, and cute. The more I talked to him, the more I wanted to get to know him, to get close to him, to be his lover. As he talked, I planned my next mode of attack, to get a kiss out of him in the parking lot.

We finished, and I was pretty proud of myself for having sampled most of the Chinese food and ignoring the American food buffet table — and not feeling overly stuffed. I got the bill, which took up the rest of my money. I always believed in tipping well.

We got up, and started toward the door. I wanted to put my hand on the small of Scott's back and, as I almost did, I heard someone say, "Faggot."

I stopped short. The restaurant was crowded now, and I couldn't tell who said it. Everyone else was bent down at their tables or booths, eating. No one was looking at me. I did a 360-degree turn to see who might have said that word. Scott had already gotten to the door, and turned around to find me still standing in the hallway.

I heard him say, "Mike."

But I stood there, listening, naturally amplifying my senses, trying to hear anyone else say that word again. If I heard it, and could determine where it came from, that person was going to wear their Chinese food and taste blood.

Scott came back from the door. "Mike, what's wrong?"

I wanted to tell him what I thought I heard. Instead, I walked slowly toward the doors, leaving him behind for a moment, before he jumped to catch up with me.

"Mike," he repeated, when we got outside. "You okay?"

"I thought I heard someone call us faggots," I told him. "I was going to go beat the living shit out of them."

Scott put a hand on my arm. From his hand, I felt something cool, like ocean waves, battering against my flames of my anger. As he touched me, I felt the fires quench. I felt quiet, not angry or even happy. Just quiet.

I took a deep, shuddering breath. "I'm sorry."

"It's all right," he said and smiled gently.

I didn't look around. I didn't check to see if it was safe to do it. I didn't care. I leaned my head down and kissed him.

The fire in my belly slowly stoked up again as I heard him make a noise of surprise, and then his hands were on my arms, as he returned the kiss. I felt only him, in my arms, my lips on his, my tongue exploring his mouth, and felt beauty and gentleness and all the things that I never felt in prison. He pulled back away from me, looking down sheepishly.

"I don't usually do that on a first date," he said.

I found that my hands were on his arms. I rubbed them up and down and let him go. "It's our second date. You paid for our first one."

He laughed. "Fair enough."

He turned around and unlocked the door for me, then walked around to his side and unlocked that door. As we drove, I put my hand on top of his on the shifter. He smiled and let me do it.

"I'll bring you to your house," he said.

"You could bring me to *your* house," I said, offering a slight mischievous grin,

He looked like he thought about it. "Not yet, Mike. Okay?"

I squeezed his hand. "Okay."

He parked in front of the house next door to mine; there were no parking spots in front of my house.

"Here you are," he said.

I nodded and turned to him. He leaned across the seat and gave me a kiss, not as passionate as the one I had given him, but he instigated it and that was enough.

I pulled away, smiling at him. "See you tomorrow?"

"If the creek don't rise," he said.

I chuckled, and exited the truck. He watched as I went up the walkway, and then pulled out, beeping the horn. I waved.

Rufus looked for a doggie bag as I entered into the apartment. Dom and Evie sat on the couch, watching TV. They both looked up after I shut the door.

"So? How'd it go?" asked Evie.

"Great," I said.

"Did you get laid?" asked Dom. Evie must have ribbed him because he went, "*Ooof.*"

"Not yet," I said, winking at him. "I'm working on it."

After I came out of the bathroom, Evie said, "This weekend we're going to my parents' house."

I stood still. "We are?"

"I want you to come, Mikey," she said. "Please."

I looked up at the ceiling and sighed. "Let me think about it."

I was distracted for the rest of the week. Did I really want to see my father and mother right now? I would have to explain to them what happened to me. How could I tell them that I summoned a demon that killed my brother and eight more people? How do I tell them that for five years I was kept in a prison? Hell, how would they react to the fact that I could use magic?

I spent a lot of time in the gym, running these thoughts over and over in my head. *What do I tell them, what do I tell them?* I didn't see Scott very much and, when I did, it was courteous and professional. He probably thought that the first date was a blow-out and, since he didn't put out, I didn't want much to do with him.

Finally, on Friday, Scott stopped the conversation we were having about the weather and asked me, "Did I do something?"

I jolted to the here and now, me standing in his store, him leaning against the counter. A light rain was falling outside, pattering on the windows, diffusing the light inside the store. The florescent light above the window had suddenly started to flicker irritatingly, so he had shut it off, casting that section of the store into the natural gray light of the overcast sky outside. Where we stood, the florescent light worked fine, and he was bathed in its fake white glow, his red hair streaked with small shiny highlights of blond here and there.

"Did you do something?" I repeated his question to gain some time.

"What's eating you? You haven't tried to kiss me since the date. Did I do something?"

I shook my head. "No, it's not you."

I turned and parked myself in the folding chair that he had gotten for me on Thursday morning, setting it up at the end of the counter. I preferred standing near him to sitting across from him.

"My sister wants me to visit my parents."

"What's wrong with that?"

"I have to tell them where I was for five years."

I sat down, tired. My brain had been working overtime trying to come up with a good excuse.

"Tell them you were in prison."

"For what? What do I tell them? Demon summoning?"

"You said tell the truth, but tell it slant. So tell them you went to prison after being forced to do magic."

I looked up at him. I blinked. "I could tell them I went to a devil worshiping cult and got arrested with them …"

The story spun on its own. It could explain why I didn't try to get a hold of them. It could explain why I hid myself for five years and only now finally decided to come back. Yes. Yes, I could handle a story like that. It wasn't too far from the truth, considering I learned most of my magic from inmates in the prison.

"You're thinking," he said, as I got the story finalized in my head.

"Yeah. Sorry. But that was a great idea." I smiled at him. "Thank you."

"Sure," he said, smiling back at me. "So I didn't do anything wrong?"

"No."

"Good because I was hoping we could go out again."

"When?"

He shrugged. "Maybe next week? I have two tickets to a play."

"A play? Really?"

"Yeah. It's *Annie*."

"*Annie?*"

"Dinner theater. I bought them this week. I was hoping to ask you yesterday, but you didn't seem like you wanted to talk about that."

"I, um, I'd love to go, sure."

"I got them for next Thursday night."

"Do I have to dress up?"

He looked me up and down. "Khakis, a polo, you know."

"I have to dress up."

He chuckled. "I suppose, if you're not used to it."

"I'm going to owe my sister big time."

That night, I told Evie and Dom about the musical. Evie looked at their budget again and figured they would be able to squeeze a shirt and pants out of it.

Saturday morning, we were in Walmart, food shopping. Lots of ramen, mac and cheese, tuna and peanut butter. Not healthy, but then, we weren't living healthy; we were just trying to live.

When we got back to their apartment, Evie made my mom's tuna casserole — one of my favorite comfort foods. Dom ate it, but I could tell he did it to make Evie happy.

When we were finished eating, he told Evie gently, "Please don't make that for me."

"I'll have to make it for Mikey."

"I like your mom's meatloaf, but this is just weird."

I stopped myself from having a third helping, knowing I'd get sick from eating too much. Instead, I patted my distended gut and sat back.

The next day, we got in the car in the early morning hours. We were supposed to drive to my parents' house for lunch.

"Sunday Dinner", as my father called it for all the years I could remember. Evie had given up correcting him.

The day was overcast, threatening to rain, but that was probably not going to happen, as I couldn't feel it in my bones.

"Dad's got no hair," said Evie, "So don't freak out. And mom, well, she got smaller and grayer."

Not sure what that meant, I sat in the back with my thoughts, going over and over in my mind what I was going to say, how I was going to explain myself. In what seemed like no time at all, we turned off the highway and into the suburbs, heading toward their gated community.

We parked in front of a condo that looked exactly like the one next to it, except the one next to it had flowers growing below its big window. Evie got out, carrying a tote bag full of RSVP's for the wedding, and a pile of papers.

She said to me, "Are you okay?"

I nodded. I wasn't going to open my mouth until I saw my parents.

Evie walked up the little walkway from the sidewalk. Dom walked beside her, his hand on the small of her back. She walked up to the front door and paused, her hand on the door handle. She looked at me through the reflection in the glass. I don't know what she saw, but she smiled at me gently, and then turned the handle, letting herself in.

"Mom," she called out as she walked in. Dom followed close behind her, and I stepped inside after they both cleared the doorway. I pulled the door closed behind us and turned to look inside the condo.

It had two floors. Where we stood was an area with a closet along the right-hand wall and a set of stairs on the left. The bottom of the set of stairs was cut in with a seat for taking off shoes and whatnot, with a little alcove to tuck the shoes into. The long hallway, with closets all the way down, led to an airy kitchen, where my mom stood at a wooden table, rolling out dough.

I stood at the entrance, looking at her. She had changed from the plump, dark-haired, dark-eyed woman that I remembered when she had left me the last morning I saw her. Her hair was gray now, short and cut to frame her face — a face now wrinkled and flabby. Everything about her seemed flabby, from her arms that looked like they had small bat wings underneath her biceps, to her stomach like a lip over her hips. She rolled the dough outward away from her across the table as I entered the room.

"Mom," I said.

Her head tilted when I spoke. Ever so slowly, she moved her head up to a straight position, looking directly at me. Her mouth dropped open, though she still held the rolling pin tight in both hands. "M … Mikey?"

I smiled. "Yeah."

She rushed around the table, still holding the rolling pin and, covered in flour, threw herself at me. I caught her — she was light as a sack of burlap and small in my arms. I hugged her, inhaling her scent, an Avon perfume smell, and the aroma of strawberries from her hair. I felt the rolling pin against my back as she hugged me so tightly that a lesser man would not have been able to breathe. Instead, I exhaled into her neck, gripping her tight enough to be strong, yet not enough to hurt her.

When she pulled away, her eyes were wet with tears. I heard the rolling pin drop to the floor. I jerked for a moment at the sudden noise.

"Oh, my God, Mikey, it's a miracle."

Not quite, but I wouldn't stop her from believing that for the moment. She stepped back, wiping her eyes with one hand, while holding onto me with the other one. I smiled down at her

— when I saw her last, she was about my height, but now, I was a good head and shoulders taller than her.

She put both hands on each of my biceps. "Mikey, my God."

I looked at Evie, who was also crying. Dom had his arm around her shoulders.

My mother said to me, "Are you all right?"

"Yeah," I said. I hugged her again. She gave me a little squeal of happiness. My own happiness threatened to choke me, flooded into my chest as it was. I fought down the tears as I squeezed her tight.

I didn't hear the door open, but I heard footsteps.

"Margie, I got the grill going."

My mother pulled away again and, still in my arms, turned to look at my father.

He was still Nordic big, but bald now, with eyes the color of the ocean choked with seaweed. He had broad shoulders and a wide chest like I remembered, but much wider in the stomach area that his t-shirt barely covered. His legs were thick like a mountain climber's, clad in the ever-present work pants that he wore on weekends. It was never jeans for him.

He stopped in the doorway opposite my mother and me, within reach of the table. He stared at me as if I was a stranger touching his wife — which I suppose I was.

"Tom," she said proudly, stepping to the my side so my father could get a better look at me. "Look who's here!"

I could tell from his face that he didn't recognize me. His eyes moved between my mother and me. My mother could tell that he was having trouble placing me.

"It's Mikey," she said, trying to help.

"*Our* Mikey?" He stared at me now. Not a grin. Still not a note of recognition.

Mom put her hand on the small of my back. "*Our* Mikey."

"Hi, Dad."

I walked toward him, a long runway of distance between him and me. His eyes were wide when I got to him, and he even took a step back. I hesitated, my arms outstretched toward him. He let me hug him, though he didn't hug me back. He smelled of lighter fluid and smoke.

He stepped away from me. "You're supposed to be dead."

The fire in my chest didn't fade; it went out completely and the dead coals fell to my feet. I dropped my arms. He turned away from me and went back outside.

"Tom!"

She glanced at me, then followed my father outside.

"Well," I said. "That's not what I expected."

"He's overwhelmed," Evie said, wiping her face with a towel she had found near the dough my mother was rolling out. She went over to where I had been standing and picked up the rolling pin.

"He didn't have to … I don't know. Say that."

Evie put her hand on my arm. We couldn't see or hear my mother through the back door. Evie rinsed off the rolling pin and placed it back on the table. At the opposite end of the table, she set up the papers, glancing at the door.

"Maybe you should go out there," Dom said to me.

"Me?"

"You're the one they're talking about."

I frowned at the door. I pulled together my courage and my will as a protection, and walked over to the door.

I could hear my mother's voice: "Don't tell me that!"

"You know that's what they said," Dad said, "They're not lying."

"You think he's lying?"

I threw open the door. They looked at me, deer in headlights. I closed the door after me, looking right at them.

"What will it take?" I asked.

"What do you mean?" asked Dad.

"You don't believe me."

Dad shifted his body from foot to foot.

"How about if I tell you something that only I would know?"

"Like what?"

I put my hands in my pockets and looked down. "Once, when I went to school on the bus, no one picked me up afterward. I was on the bus the entire time. Nobody came and got me until after the bus got to the depot, and you came to get me." I raised my eyes back toward him. "I was so scared, I wet my pants, and you didn't want me to sit in the car because you said it would smell like piss. Do you remember that?"

What did I expect? Him to suddenly burst into tears and run at me and hug me and kiss me and say he was so sorry to not trust me? Did I expect him to say, "C'mere, son", and throw his arms open for me?

No. I should have expected what he did.

"Yes, I remember," he said coldly. He turned away from me, looking at the grill. "I suppose you're who you say you are."

"Tom," said Mom. "Give him a hug."

My father shrugged and didn't move.

I felt the fire get stoked right up again, only this time it was a furnace of rage.

"This is bullshit." I stormed over to him and got in his face, intersecting myself between him and the grill. "You don't know what I went through, and you know what? I don't need your damn approval anymore."

He slapped me. "Don't use that language."

"Screw you," I said, and shoved him. I was a lot stronger than him, and he wasn't expecting it.

He staggered back, while my mother yelled at me.

"Mikey!"

My father's eyes narrowed. "Get out of my house."

"What is your problem? I'm your *son*, for God's sake."

"You're no son of mine. Get out of my house or I'll call the cops!"

"Tom, Mikey. Stop!" My mother started to cry.

"Now see what you've done," my father said. "Get out."

My hands were clenched into fists at my side. I had the spell to set the man on fire was ready at the tip of my tongue. He was coated with lighter fluid. He'd go up like a candle.

"Both of you, stop it!" my mother wailed.

I threw open the door to the house, went inside, slammed the door shut, and walked through the kitchen. Evie called me, but I ignored her as I walked out of the kitchen, down the hall, and out the front door.

I kept walking.

My old neighborhood wasn't close to this gated community, but I walked there anyway. It took me an hour to reach the playground I had romped in when I was a kid.

It was a skeleton of a playground. Two triangular pairs of metal bars stood embedded in the ground, connected by a bar on the top. No swings were threaded through the s-links at the top of the metal bar. A large metal climbing pyramid had garbage piled inside it. Monkey bars were missing links. A bench had a huge hole in it, with trash and leaves strewn underneath it.

I sat down on the bench. I was furious and sad, both at the same time. My phone rang again, for the fifth time. I sighed, debating on whether or not to answer it this time. I pulled it out and glanced at the number: Dom.

I flipped it open. "Yeah."

"Where are you?"

I looked around at the graveyard that had once been a playground. "Where we used to play when we were kids."

"You want me to come get you?" Dom asked. "Your mom's upset."

"When my father decides to apologize." ... *for all the years he treated me like shit.* That time with the school bus wasn't the first.

"Yeah, well, I'll buy ice skates when that happens."

"Are you guys leaving?"

"Not yet. Evie wanted me to make sure you were okay. They're still doing the seating plans, more or less, between your mom's crying jags."

"Call me when you're going to leave." I sighed. "Tell her I'm sorry."

"I will, man." He hung up. So did I, pocketing the phone.

I sat and watched some people walk by with their dogs, ignoring me, letting their dogs crap on the field that I used to watch Phil play Little League on. I had been too embarrassed to try out. I could almost see myself out in the field. When a fly ball would come my way, I ducked. When I picked up a ball, I threw it underhand, and it always fell short of its destination. When I ran bases, I was too slow and dainty, sometimes tripping over the base.

I wasn't Phil, who barreled into bases, threw a mean fastball, and physically shoved people out of the way to get the fly ball.

I wasn't Phil, who played all the sports, got the girls, passed his classes, and graduated high school with a varsity letter jacket.

I wasn't Phil, who helped Dad around the house, who hefted groceries from the car to the house, who could have gone to college on a scholarship.

I wasn't Phil, who I hated, and was so jealous of that I wished him dead — and he did die, right in front of me.

"Hey, man, whatchu looking' for?"

I snapped out of my reverie to look up at a skinny dark man in a bulky jacket, his hands thrust deep into his pockets. His eyes were moved constantly, and he seemed to be shivering in that heavy coat.

"Nothing," I said.

"I got what you need," he said. "Ten or twenty?"

"Nothing," I said again.

"Then get outta my spot. You're scarin' away people."

I raised an eyebrow and stood up. "You mean to tell me you're selling drugs here? In this playground?"

He barked. "Shit, man, this ain' been no playground for *years.*"

Amazing what five years could do.

I started to walk away. I turned back for a moment and watched the guy, hunched over, looking at something on his arm. I kept walking.

I went by my old house. It was a triple-decker, similar to the kind of house Evie lived in, except my family had lived on the first floor, and my parents had been the landlords. Loud rap music came from the house two doors down, but no one seemed to mind. Some of the cars had Jesus pictures on the headlights; rosary beads hung from their rear-view mirrors.

I definitely started feeling a little uncomfortable, so I called Dom. I walked to the end of the street, to the main street, while I waited for him to answer. I could see Karin's Kountry Kitchen on the corner. I crossed the street to it, but it was closed. It looked like it had been closed for a long time.

"Hey," Dom answered.

"When are you guys heading out?"

"A little bit. Evie told me where you are."

"I moved," I said. "I'm at Karin's Kountry Kitchen. I'll be there."

"Give me fifteen."

It was more like twenty minutes, but he got there. Alone. I climbed into the car, relieved.

"You okay, man?" he asked as he drove away. I didn't look back. My neighborhood was gone.

"Yeah," I said. "My mom's upset?"

"She thinks you ran away again."

"I guess I did," I said, as he got back on the highway. "I almost hit him."

"I probably wouldn't have blamed you if you did. He's always been a jerk."

"Even to you?"

He chuckled. "Especially to me. I think I was the surrogate son that he lost."

"I'm sorry."

"Not your fault. He's probably been a worse jerk since Phil died. But that doesn't give him the excuse to be a jerk, you know what I mean?"

"Yeah." The exit was a short distance away. What had taken me an hour to walk took him less than fifteen minutes to get back.

He parked the car in front of the house. "You should at least go see your mom."

I nodded, then got out of the car. When I went back into the house, the kitchen table had been cleaned off. Evie and Mom were sitting there, talking. I heard the TV in the other room. That's where Dad was going to be.

Mom looked up at me and smiled weakly. Her eyes were puffy. "Mikey," she said. I bent down and kissed her cheek. She grabbed a hold of my hand. "Please don't be mad at him."

"I *am* mad at him," I said, pulling away, not looking in the other room where he probably sat with a beer, watching ESPN.

"It was easier for him to think you were dead," she said, and my heart broke a little. "Give him some time."

"Easier to think I was dead? He already thought I was worthless, so why not put me in the grave?"

"Mikey, please." My mother's eyes pleaded with me. "It's Phil. He never got over it."

I was sick of her excuses for him. Evie had gotten up and looked ready to go.

I said, "I have to go, Mom."

"Will you be back?"

I glanced at Evie, who nodded. "Sure, Mom," I said, giving her another kiss on the cheek. "For you, I'll come back."

CHAPTER FOURTEEN

BATTLES

THE NEXT WEEK WAS QUIET, for the most part. I got my fancy clothes, and went with Scott to see *Annie* on Thursday. I'm not a fan of musicals, but Scott seemed to be, as he sang some of the songs along with the cast. *He has a good voice*, I thought. When we left, he was singing, "Tomorrow".

"What?" he asked me, when he finished the song.

I must have been grinning like a goofball. "You going to serenade me?"

"Do you want me to?"

"Pick something different, though."

He started into "It's the Hard Knock Life". I gave him a playful shove, and he stopped, laughing.

"What do you want to hear? I take requests."

"Not show tunes."

He looked pained. "You wound me, sir."

I put my arm around his shoulders. "I'd like to hear you sing in the shower."

"With you in it?"

"That's the point."

He ducked out from under my arm as we headed back to his truck.

Now, usually, I would have noticed if someone was watching us. He obviously felt someone watching us, or he wouldn't have done that. I looked around, the hairs on the back of my neck pricked up. It was just the normal crowd coming out of the dinner theater, nothing different. That's not to say that the crowd coming out of the theater was gay. But I thought what I had done was harmless enough.

We walked to the truck in silence, him humming something to himself, probably another song from the play. I was cautious though, my senses searching out for whatever might be out there. Again, I felt nothing unusual.

When we got into the truck, he leaned over the seat to me and kissed my cheek. I turned my head, grabbed his head, and kissed him a bit more passionately. He uttered a small noise, like a moan with a gasp. I released him, and he pulled away.

"I'd better take you back to your home," he said. "Or I'll do something I might regret."

"I don't think you'd regret it," I told him.

He shook his head. "I can't sleep with you."

I sat back. "Why?"

He started the truck and eased out of the parking spot. When he got out onto the street from the parking lot, he said, "I've always slept with the bad boys and it never works out in the end."

"I'm different," I said.

He kept looking in the rear-view mirror. He turned in the opposite direction from my house, heading toward the northern part of Pawtucket. "You're an ex-con," he said. "You don't have a job. You're living with your sister."

"I'll get a job, if that's what's holding you back," I said. "And I'll get my own apartment after they get married."

He looked in the rear-view mirror again. He looked worried. "We're being followed."

I turned around. I could only see headlights. "Pull into the parking lot over there," I said.

He did. The headlights followed, and then blocked the entrance.

"Great," Scott said.

We faced a closed convenience store, with no other exit out of the parking lot.

I heard a car door slam. Scott looked in the side mirror, his hands tightly gripping the steering wheel. I couldn't see what he could see.

Then I saw a man at his door. The window was closed. The man rapped on it. Scott looked straight ahead and did not look like he was going to open the window. I put my hand on the handle of the door, intending to leap out and find out what this guy's problem was.

He rapped again. I heard the click of a lock. I tried the door; it was locked from the inside.

"Scott," I said, tugging on the door handle.

In the dim light, I saw him shake his head. "No."

He looked in the side view mirror again. When he did, I saw the man outside take a step back, out of my line of sight in the window. I thought he wore glasses, but I wasn't sure.

"Scott, let me out."

I had a spell at hand, something that would light up the area. Then we could at least see who we were up against.

"No," he repeated.

I heard a thump against the window. Scott turned to look at it, making a noise of surprise. I saw the man outside punch the window again, thumping against the glass. Scott ducked, put the truck in gear, and slammed on the gas. Except he pulled too hard on the clutch, causing the truck to lurch forward, and then stall.

"Shit!"

I yanked on the door handle. It opened this time, and I jumped out. The man walked toward us, but saw me and turned his body in my direction. He raised his arm.

I ran back around the truck, thinking he had a gun. I wasn't wrong. *Bang!* — a scream, and a loud *clink*. I looked over the hood of the truck to no longer see Scott in the driver's seat, but the front window shattered from a spot in the middle of the window.

"Scott!"

"I'm okay!" he shouted, and threw open his door.

Another loud *bang!*, closer this time, and I got out from in front of the truck, running to Scott's door. He slammed the door shut as I came around.

"God dammit," I muttered, pulling him into my arms.

He was hot, full of energy. I drew on it, combining it with my will, and threw my hand up in the air, sending a shock of light above the truck that flashed about five feet above our heads. Another *bang!*, and I saw who was shooting.

Of all people, I didn't expect this.

Marty's horn-rimmed glasses were tilted on his face, but he didn't seem to care. He advanced on us, holding the gun out with one hand.

I pushed Scott away, yelling, "Run!"

He stumbled away from me, but he didn't run away. Instead, he ran at Marty at full tilt, avoiding the gun and tackling him. The gun fell out of Marty's hand, bouncing off the asphalt, and landing somewhere under the truck.

Scott stood in a boxer's crouch and jabbed at Marty. He hit him in the nose, making Marty stumble back, holding it. Scott advanced, keeping himself small and nimble, jabbing again and again at Marty's face. Marty put his hands up to cover his head to protect himself. I tried to find the gun, but couldn't see it in the shadow of the underside of the truck.

Marty made a whining noise, and then reached out to grab at Scott. Scott danced back, out of arm's length. I ducked under the truck and swept my arm around in the dark, feeling for the gun. I still couldn't find it.

Scott stayed in his boxer's stance while Marty stood in the middle of the parking lot, bleeding from his nose. He grinned through the blood, and gazed at Scott. He raised his hand and spoke in a horrible language that I didn't know, and then he took a step forward.

Scott went flying across the parking lot, smashing into the car's front. I heard him crunch into the metal followed by the crash of glass.

"You bastard!" I screamed.

Marty turned to me. He stretched out his hand. The gun flew out from under the car and landed in his hand with a smack. He turned the gun on me.

"I like this boom stick," Marty said in a deep and gravelly voice that I knew as Belial. "Causes such destruction." He aimed it toward Scott.

"Stop!" I yelled, and ran at him.

Marty flicked his hand up, swatting a fly. This time, I went flying, slamming into the grille of the truck. Pain ran up my side, and I couldn't breathe for a minute.

"Belial!" I didn't know how, but that demon had gone into Marty, not back to Hell. That's why the bastard had smiled when I tried to banish him. Grimalkin had either lied or been misinformed. Either way, I was dealing with Belial now. Belial, who raised the gun at Scott.

He fired, and I heard glass explode. I could see Scott in the dim light, scrambling to run behind the car, using it for cover.

Now Belial turned to me. I had gotten to my feet, getting ready to run and tackle him, but he now pointed the gun in my direction. I stood up, holding my hands up.

"Belial, let's make a deal."

He fired at me. The shot missed and blew out the windshield behind me instead.

Sirens.

Keep him talking, I thought.

"Belial. Don't you want power? Strength?" I tapped my chest.

He shot at me again. It hit the grille penetrating the radiator beyond, just barely missing my thigh.

A screech of tires behind me.

"They'll kill you, you know," I said. "Destroy you, and I will send you back to Hell."

He moved the gun. It was now aimed at my chest.

"I'm inviting you," I said. I could handle him. I could do the ritual myself later and send him back to Hell. Of course, he might take me with him. But I didn't want him to kill Scott.

"Did Marty invite you?"

Red lights flashed in the windows of the closed store at the end of the parking lot.

"Marty was not in his body anymore," he said. "The vessel was empty."

He pulled the trigger.

I dove to one side. The bullet bit my upper arm, slicing through my new shirt, scratching the flesh, and then continued through the truck's open windshield.

"I found his blood in the soil. I returned to him to find him empty."

Belial tracked me with the gun. I ran down the side of the truck to try to get to the back of it. There, I could see a police cruiser, its lights flashing, and a cop on the opposite side of an open door, pointing his gun at me.

"Put the gun down!" the cop shouted.

"I don't have a gun!" I turned back to see Belial raise the gun at me and pull the trigger again.

This time, he got me in the right shoulder. It felt like my shoulder had been blasted out of its socket. The force of the bullet sent me spiraling to the ground. I heard a scream. I think it was me. I fell hard to the ground just behind the back of the truck.

Belial advanced, grinning.

Another car arrived, then another, and soon the air was full of flashing lights. But Belial was going to shoot me before the cops shot him, and I was a sitting duck. I tried to reach up with my left hand to the bumper to haul myself up, so that I could at least be standing when I died.

"Boy Wizard," he said, aiming the gun right at my head. "Now you die."

As a last resort, with my left hand, I made the sign of protection and visualized a bubble in front of me, a barrier that nothing could get past.

Then I heard someone yell. Scott ran up from behind Belial and slammed him in the back of the head with what looked like a crowbar. Belial stumbled forward, firing the gun into the asphalt, barely missing my leg. I crawled back, finally grabbing the bumper and pulling myself upward, while I scrambled with my feet.

Belial put a hand on the back of his head and pulled it away, covered with blood. He looked at me, grinned, and collapsed to the ground.

And jumped into me.

⊛   ⊛   ⊛

It was everything I ever wanted.

Power. Strength. Fury. The knowledge that if I surrendered my will, I could do anything.

He brought me back to when I had first summoned him: April 15, 1995, a week before my 13th birthday. That day I was forced to come out. The day I was beaten so bad that the school bus monitor had to walk me to the door.

"Is your mother home?" the monitor asked.

"Yeah," I told her, and let myself in.

I could barely see out of one eye. I went upstairs to my room. Instead of crawling into bed and crying about it, I grabbed my "Aunt Jane's overnight bag" that I hadn't used in a year. Inside were some items, but not all of the things, needed to summon a spirit, as Aunt Jane called them.

I went into the garage, the largest spot I could think of that was enclosed, and drew the circles on the concrete floor in chalk. One circle for the summoning; one circle for the protection.

With chalk, I drew Belial's symbol in the circle next, then stepped into my protective circle and cast the spell. He appeared, as if waiting for me to call him.

"How may I serve you?"

"Kill everyone who ever hurt me."

I remember him laughing, but in this replay, he didn't. He only bowed his head. The next scene I saw was the last moment I saw Phil alive, pulling into the driveway while I stood at the

236

door, my backpack over my shoulder. I had clothes, food, my birthday money.

"Where the Hell you think you're going?" he yelled at me. "What's this I heard in school you're a faggot?"

"Phil, I —"

He raised his right hand, a big paw that was meant for catching footballs and hauling sacks of rice, like he did at the store he worked at. He raised it like my father often raised his hand to me, to hit me in the mouth, the head, the face. He raised it — and it was the last thing he did.

He fell down right at my feet.

I ran. I ran in this replay, too, running for my life, running to Aunt Jane's, but not getting there, instead running into the prison courtyard, where all the men and women stared at me like foxes looking at the fattest chicken. Predatory eyes. Licking chops. Hands motioning for me to come to them.

Hands that would beat me senseless in the shower, in the hall, even in my own cell. Malachi was tall, broad, and huge, with white hair, and a beard down to his chest, He beat me nearly every day — either he, or one of his "lieutenants". No one came to my rescue, not the guards, not another inmate.

Only Grimalkin.

Malachi had wrestled me to the floor of the shower and shoved my face into a puddle. I tried to turn my face as best I could, to get air, to scream, but I didn't have enough air for that. Just enough to breathe the warm water. The tiles were cold on my cheek, but warmed under my shame.

I didn't scream. It wouldn't matter. The rest of the block did nothing, the guards did nothing, and no one was going to save me. I cried.

And Belial showed it to me again.

Mike, don't leave me!

Evie? Evie's voice invaded my dream, even while Malachi loomed over me, his foot on my back, the hot water peppering my skin.

And, at that moment, as had happened in real life, Grimalkin appeared and whispered the spell that had worked, even beyond the magic-neutralizing runes all over the prison. I used the spell to gain strength to throw Malachi across the room and into the wall on the other side.

This is a dream. Belial is trying to control me.

I forced the dream to explode into shards of black glass, and I felt power coming from outside of me, feeding my own will. It wasn't the same power and strength that Belial gave me, but something purer. It felt like cold spring water on a hot summer morning, refreshing and clean. I grabbed a hold of that as best I could, catching water cascading from a waterfall.

The dream resolved itself.

This time I was at the garage where I had summoned Belial in the first place. He stood there in the middle of the circle, looking shocked to discover that he was there.

I raised my hands and began the banishing ritual, "In the name of ADONAI …"

"You can't banish me!" he roared. "I am part of you now."

I ignored his statement and I kept going.

"… let each of you return …"

When I finished the words, I watched a black circle appear in the circle where he stood. He sank into it, like being dragged into quicksand. He clawed at the edge of the circle as I began the first chapter of Genesis.

"You will always have me," he yelled at me. "I will always be with you."

"No," said Grimalkin, standing outside of the circle. His arms crossed his hairy red chest, his hooves just outside of the circle, as he watched Belial sink lower and lower into the floor. "No," Grimalkin repeated. "I will."

Belial clawed at the edge of the barrier, sending shocks of black electricity through the sphere that formed the boundary of the circle. The black inky substance that Belial stood in slowly swallowed him up, taking as long as quicksand. He continued to try frantically to grab hold of something — anything — to stop himself from sinking into it.

I finished the first chapter of the Book of Genesis. Only a single ripple of ink remained on the circle. And then, nothing.

Grimalkin sighed and looked over to me. "Return," he said, with a wave of his hand.

I snapped backwards like I was on a rubber band, and then I slammed into awareness.

First, I heard the beeps. Then the breathing between the beeps. Then I felt someone holding my hand. I gave it a squeeze.

I heard a gasp. I opened my eyes to see I was in a hospital bed, with tubes and wires trailing away me. I now heard the bustle of the hospital, and heard someone get up from a chair. I looked over.

"Scott," I said, and gave him a heartfelt smile of relief.

"Mike," he said, tears welling up in his eyes. He was smiling, too.

That's when the pain in my shoulder hit me and I grunted. "Oh, crap, how long have I been here?"

"They brought you down from surgery three hours ago. I called your sister. They just went out for something to eat."

"I'm glad you're here," I said, squeezing his hand again.

He looked down. "I tried to heal you. Send you good vibes?"

"You did. Thank you."

At that, he grinned even more.

And then Evie came in with Dom. "Oh, Mikey!" she cried, and ran over to my side.

Scott let go of my hand while Evie grabbed my head and kissed me.

"Ow," I said, feeling a tearing pain shoot through my shoulder.

"I'm sorry!" She let go of me. "You scared me, Mikey! What were you doing getting shot?"

"It's not like I planned it!"

"You could have been killed."

I looked over to Scott. "So could he." To Scott, I asked, "Are you all right?"

He nodded. "Yeah, just a few scrapes. Nothing broken."

"Is Marty dead?"

"The guy who shot you?" Scott seemed confused for a moment. He rubbed the back of his head. "I think so. I don't know. I've been with you the whole time."

"Scott told us what happened," said Evie, sitting down, but holding my left hand.

Then the nurse came in. "Hello, Mr. LeBonte. How are you feeling?" He was pretty cute, but I realized I only had eyes for Scott.

"Like my shoulder's been blown off."

He chuckled. "It almost was. But we have one of the best surgeons in the country for that sort of thing, so he did the best he could to repair it. How's the pain right now, on a scale of 1-10?"

"Seven? Eight?"

He nodded. "You'll probably be on morphine for a couple of days until the pain subsides, and then on an oral medication. But I'm not the doctor." He noted something in the computer and then said, "Once we get you a bed, you'll be on a morphine pump."

"Oh, boy, I'll be high." I saw the concerned look on Evie's face. "But I don't really want that."

"Don't worry, if you don't want to be addicted, you won't be. We're just waiting for a bed to open upstairs. You'll be with us for a few days."

"A few days" turned out to be three, once they found out I had no insurance. They sent me home in a sling, and with pain medication that I refused to take.

Scott stayed with me and visited constantly for those three days. When I got out of the hospital, he called me every few hours to make sure I was okay. It took about a week, but I finally walked down to his store.

He jumped up when I entered. My arm was still in a sling, but it felt a lot better. I was getting used to the pain.

"How are you feeling?" he asked, while he got a folding chair from the back.

"Much better," I said. "I have to take my arm out of this sling, but I don't know when I can work with it."

"You need to go to physical therapy," he said. "I know a good one in the area."

"I don't have any money."

"I'll send you."

"Scott, I can't ask you for that."

"Mike, I have enough money to send you for a couple of weeks of PT. They'll give you exercises and help you develop those muscles back again." He looked steadily at me. "There is a catch."

I knew there would be. "What is it?"

"You bring me to your sister's wedding."

I laughed. "Can you get a suit in three weeks?"

"I can get a suit tonight," he said with a chuckle. "Well?"

I walked over to him, stood over him, and looked deep into his bright green eyes.

"You got yourself a deal."

ABOUT THE AUTHOR

Find out more about the world of L. A. Jacob at
Grimalkin's Grimoire (grimaulkin.com).

YOU MIGHT ALSO ENJOY

HOMECOMING
A War Mage Novel

BY JAKE LOGAN

Even wizards in the U.S. armed forces have to go home some time.

Best Intentions
Book One of the Glass Bottles Series

by J Dark

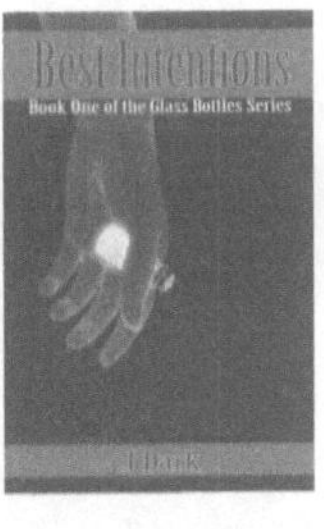

When your past is left undone, it will come find you.

Available from Paper Angel Press in
hardcover, trade paperback, and ebook editions.
paperangelpress.com